LAKE MAGIC—

Snow-Eyes was falling forward—or backward? . . . She kicked to find a footing, grabbed at air and tried to break her tumble with her shoulder but . . . she had no arms. They were shrunken, mere fingerless stumps. Her legs were gone, too. Yet, she had something there in their place, something thick and long and powerful . . . a finned tail. Where her arms had been, pectoral fins grew. The air tasted metallic, tainted with iron . . . except, she was not breathing air. Her chest did not expand and contract with the exercise of lungs, instead, gills opened and closed. She had no voice.

Floating, suspended above the earth, voiceless, legless, and blind, she was trapped in a spell beyond her comprehension. . . .

SNOW-EYES

by

Stephanie A. Smith

DAW BOOKS, INC.

DONALD A. WOLLHEIM, PUBLISHER

1633 Broadway, New York, NY 10019

First DAW Printing, July 1988

1 2 3 4 5 6 7 8 9

PRINTED IN THE U.S.A.

*For UKL and VNM,
without whom this tale
would not have been written;
and for the women
of the red house.*

Contents

SNOW

I am living in the Isle of Wise
and there is nothing wrong

The wind drives along
the blessing of the skies.

O bread of heaven, storm
of transformation, change

Sorrow to something strange!

In the cold one keeps warm.

—Ursula K. Le Guin
from *Wild Angels*

1

The Wishing Stone

THE CARPENTER always dressed his youngest child in black. He called her Snow-Eyes, even though her birth-name was Amarra and even though, when she was young, her eyes were not pale at all, but dark like the clothes she wore, as black as new-turned earth under the sun. In the northern Kieldings of Gueame, where time, during the winter, seems to pass more slowly than in the south, many wondrous tales are spoken of the woman grown, Amarra Snow-Eyes. But this is a southern story, and it is about the child.

Later tales seldom tell that Snow-Eyes had an elder brother and sister. Their names, lest they be forgotten, were Edan and Edarra. It is said that their mother died when they were both young. In the years we speak of, they lived together with their sister and their father, Paudan Nie, in the family house near the shores of Lake Wyessa, in a valley west of Woodmill Kield.

During the wet, southern summers, Paudan and his eldest child, Edarra, would travel about the Kielding, villa to villa, with their tools—awls, files, sanders and knives—to make chairs of hardwood or tables, short yew boxes for sweets or bamboo cylinders to hold mending needles or anything else they were asked. Paudan was known, too, for his painting. Most often he would make signs for Kield marketeers, although every now and then the Drake Villae, the ruler of Woodmill, would commission a portrait.

Because of her father's and sister's absence in the summer, Snow-Eyes often felt lonely. She and Edan had each other, but without all four people, the house was so quiet it made her sad. That is why she loved the winter. During the snowy season the carpenter and his eldest would stay home, and Edan did not have to work such long hours. And sometimes, as they all sat together after the day's last meal, Paudan would whittle. Other times, he would take out his battered tin paintbox and embellish his whittled animal figurines with eyes, so that the thumb-tall bears, owls and mice might seem alive to his children.

One of these winter evenings, as Edarra cleared the table of dishes, she said, "Tithe is due soon."

No one answered her; no one spoke. She took a brand from the kitchen's hearth and lit two more floorcandles so that her little sister, who sat at the table before a book, might have enough light by which to practice her letters. The fire in the hearth crackled; the wind outside the house whistled.

Paudan opened the lid of his paintbox. He lifted out two figures—a bear and an owlet. He sighed. "There is no time when the tithe is not due." He dipped one of his smallest brushes into a pan of water.

The brother, Edan, added a wedge of wood to the fire and then began to sweep the flagstones clean of ash and soot. The rasping of the frayed straw bristles against the floor and the crackle from the fire were the only sounds. Snow-Eyes glanced down at her book again. The story Paudan had given her to learn told about a hidden staircase in an ancient place where moss covered the walls and—

Paudan said, "Can we not pay the tithe?"

"Oh, yes," said Edan.

"Barely," snapped Edarra in such a harsh tone that Snow-eyes dared not look up from the page of her book. She put her hands in her lap and stared at the bluish letters on the page before her.

Edan tucked the broom back in its corner and walked over to his youngest sister. He put one hand upon her head, and she gave him a quick, uncertain smile. He grinned. Glancing over to where Edarra stood beside the hearth, he said, "I shall carry the tithe to Woodmill, if you wish."

She shook her head and sat down on a stool. "That isn't what's troubling me. I have heard—" She paused.

"What? What have you heard?"

Again she shook her head. "I shall go to Woodmill. There is someone to whom I must speak."

"Who?" said Edan. He pulled another stool near to her and he sat.

Paudan shut his paintbox. "To whom must you speak?"

"The Drake Villae. You know she wishes to have the Lake Mother's portrait, Paudan. I think we ought to give it to her, in the place of this season's tithing. The winter is long. The tithe grows heavier. We shan't have enough to eat, I fear."

"No," said Paudan. "No. We must find another way." He dropped his paintbrush onto the table.

"But," said Edarra, "if we could only save just a little this season! The portrait—"

"No!"

Snow-Eyes felt tears smart under her eyelids; the words of the story book wavered. Her father and her sister did not argue often, but they had been arguing about the same portrait only a day before.

"No," she muttered to herself, echoing her father. "That picture is *my* picture . . ."

It hung in the largest room of their villa and it was precious to the little girl; the work of Paudan's brush, it showed a dark-haired woman with almond-shaped, silver eyes. The child had become entranced by the woman's face. She would sit in the corner of the room and whisper to herself all manner of make-believe in which the woman, who was named the Lake Mother, might step down out of the frame into life.

Whenever Edarra spoke ill of the picture, which she often did, Snow-Eyes was hurt and frightened that her father would someday give the woman with the silver eyes away to the Drake.

"Paudan," said Edarra.

He stood up. "No! Understand me. That painting belongs to myself and no one else shall have it, until I die. It is all that I have left—" He glanced at Snow-Eyes and then, without another word, left the kitchen.

Edarra sighed. "Stubborn," she said as she put a handful of tea leaves into the enameled pot of steaming water. "It would be better for him to forget—"

"Let him be," said Edan gently. "He's getting older, and that painting is probably the last one he will ever do. You know how stiff and painful his fingers are."

Edarra nodded. "I start for Woodmill tomorrow. Snow-Eyes? Would you like to come along with me?"

Startled, the child glanced up from the book. "Yes—oh, yes!" she cried.

Edarra smiled a small, small, curving smile as she poured the tea into two cups. She handed one to her brother.

"Paudan has agreed?" he asked.

"Yesterday." Edarra leaned toward her sister. "I have already packed a knapsack for you. But you must promise to carry it for yourself and to do as I say."

"I promise," said the child.

"Good. When you've finished your lesson there, then you ought to go to bed and sleep. We leave at first light."

Snow-Eyes nodded and put her hands flat on the pages of the book. She sat up straight and stared intently at the story, frowning. Her brother chuckled.

After she had discovered that the tale told of a terrible man and his dark, dank, mossy villa, which was also a tomb, and of another man who was trapped in the tomb, she stole a glance at her sister and brother. They sat beside the fire, sharing their tea. Edan and Edarra seemed so much older than she, so much wiser, though in truth they were not so much more than children themselves. Both were tall and fair. Edan was the darker, with freckle-peppered skin and thin, pale lips. Edarra was the taller and had heavy-muscled shoulders, from all the swimming she liked to do. Her long hair was a squash-blossom color to Edan's chestnut, and she wore it braided in a roll at the nape of her neck, while he wore his long and free. Snow-Eyes wished that they would talk to her more often than they did. She wished she were older. As she glanced from face to face, the two faces of her siblings cut sharply in halves by the fire's light, shaded on one side, blushed ruddy on the other, she wondered why Edarra seldom laughed. Edan could laugh. Edan—he was usually the quietest of them all. He knew how to patch clothes so that the patchwork did not show and he tended to all the needs of their flat-roofed villa and tilled the land. He was the one who worried most over the potatoes and carrots, the beans and cabbages, the one who had raised a flock of chickens and who worked the longest hours, living, more so than any of his family, by the sun's course, seldom lingering late beside a floorcandle's light, as did Snow-Eyes. Edan, the practical one, could be teased into chasing his little sister around a table or across the backyard, scattering chickens and reaching out to tickle her silly. Cajoled, he might snatch up a whittled owlet and make it fly down the length of the kitchen table to pounce onto her shoulder and tweak her ear.

But Edarra walked too grimly for running, laughed too seldom for giggles. She was solemn. Snow-Eyes puzzled over this, staring across the room.

Edarra caught the child's dark eyes fixed upon her. Frowning again, she said, "Off to bed, now."

Snow-Eyes shut up the book and got down from the bench. "Good eve," she said.

"Good eve, little one," replied Edan.

Edarra nodded.

Snow-Eyes left the kitchen and walked up the hall. Like most southern Kielding villas, the little flat-roofed house where Amarra Snow-Eyes was born was square. In the middle of the square was an atrium garden and in the middle of the garden, a wishing stone stood. On all four sides of the atrium a columned hall had been built, onto which each room in the villa opened, either by door or an arch. Snow-Eyes headed around the hall. As she came to the front room's ornamented door, she stopped and thought to go inside to peek at the portrait of the Lake Mother. But just then she heard Edan and Edarra walking around the garden behind her, so she ran to her own room and hopped into bed. A moment later Edarra came in. In the darkness the older girl undressed quickly and covered herself with two blankets.

That night, Snow-Eyes dreamt that she was exploring the villa, as she was wont to do in the wintertime. She climbed up the rickety bamboo ladder to the flat roof where blue crowns nested. There she found a clutch of speckled eggs. She stole one of the eggs, and cradling it in the palm of her hand, she hurried back down the ladder, across the atrium garden, past the shiny, black wishing stone and then down the steps to the root cellar, down where the mice lived in dark corners and where she would sometimes join them, pretending bewitchment, child in mouse's hide but regrettably tailless. There she chased the shadows away, getting her black pants full of dust. When all the shadows were gone, she placed the egg on the white, white floor. It began to hatch—

"Snow-Eyes?" said someone.

The child woke with a start. Edarra stood over her.

"Are you awake?" said the elder sister.

"Now I am."

"You must get dressed, if you want to join me."

Snow-Eyes flung back her blue blanket and dashed after her sister, leaving her dream unfinished and the egg unhatched. Bundled into a thick woollen jacket and heavy trousers, her head and neck swathed in a black shawl, she did as Edarra told her: ate a bowl of porridge, went to the outhouse, shouldered her pack. Together, yawning, they tramped through the chilly dawn across a dewy field and through the forest, waking lake gillians as they went down to the shores of Lake Wyessa where the family's coracle was tied up. Rowing themselves across the lake and onto the wide, flat river called the Middlemost, they soon came to Woodmill Kield.

Snow-Eyes wanted to lie down and sleep— but she could not because . . . there! There was the gateway of the Kield and so many people; many, many more people than she had ever seen. The walls of Woodmill stood higher than a man's height and were blackened with bitumen. The gate, wooden and iron-bound, was open. The child saw a cart at the gateway. It was similar to the one they had at home for hauling straw, but it was pulled not by a bullock, but by a man, and it carried a woman. As Snow-Eyes and Edarra walked into the Kield, the child could not stand still. Restless, she tugged at her sister's sleeve.

"Ho—" said Edarra. "Behave."

But Snow-Eyes could not behave. Everything was so confusing and beautiful to her. The villas with their windowless walls huddled near the gate, their wooden doors carved with the same sort of animals that Paudan carved for his children—owls, bears, bullocks, lambs and frogs—and the doors were brightly painted in sky blue or brassy yellow. In the crisp air and new sunshine, the colors seemed sharp and biting to the child as if they were alive—just as a hearth flame seems to live—as if they could dance off the wood to wrap themselves around her.

Two women dressed in felt trousers and identical yellow cloaks nodded at Edarra, who bowed her head in return. Snow-Eyes blushed. Who were those great ladies, who could live in such a fantastic place as this Woodmill? She tugged at Edarra's hand and said, "Who—?"

Instead of answering, Edarra yanked Snow Eyes by her arm swiftly to the side of the road. The child yelped; so sharply had she been pulled that her arm felt wrenched from its socket. She glanced over her shoulder— what awful thing were they fleeing? It was another cart, towed by a young man. It raced so close to them that Snow-Eyes felt the whiffle of wind it made. She saw that the cart was curtained so that whatever or whomever was inside was hidden. A bright copper cage was chained to its railing.

"Look!" she cried.

Edarra shook her head. "Don't be a nuisance. You've seen an owl before." She lifted the child off the ground.

The painted cart, strung with brass bells and adorned with its caged owlet, rattled away toward the Kielding gate. The cage swung perilously close to the wheels, so close that the child was sure the cage would be broken and the owlet crushed. She held her breath. But nothing happened.

Edarra walked through the marketeers' quadrangle. From the vantage of her sister's shoulder, Snow-Eyes peered avidly at the Kielding. Everything seemed so big! The twelve pointed roofs of the Drake Villae's home loomed over the streets and cast deep shadows on the quadrangle's pavement. Long wooden tables fanned out before the foot of one entryway, their white awnings decorated with crimson tassels. The quadrangle was terribly noisy to the child, who was more accustomed to the silence of lakeside fields and forests. She put her head down on her sister's shoulder, as Edarra threaded her way past fruitiers and egg hagglers, toward the main door of the twelve-roofed Kield Hall.

Edarra had come to pay tithe to the Drake Villae, the ruler of all Woodmill, she who was named powerful and wise. Snow-Eyes was curious to see the Drake, but she knew that the Drake was seldom seen or heard, and that she expressed her wishes through her many ci'esti—men and women whom she had chosen to train as her assistants. Yet Edarra told Paudan she would speak to the Drake about the portrait of the Lake Mother . . . Snow-Eyes wondered.

Ignoring the enticements of the market,

the sisters went inside the Hall. They were ushered by a chatty doorkeeper from the antechamber into a wide barrel-vaulted room. Stone pillars supported the vaults and the scooped ceiling had been painted with scenes of dancing, of deaths and of victories in battle—all strange happenings to Snow-Eyes, who knew nothing of dance or of war. Edarra walked over to a circle of seven stone benches in the middle of the room, where a group of people sat.

Snow-Eyes climbed out of her sister's arms and stood staring at the painted procession of animals above her. The animals were roped to one another and wore thick collars around their necks. They each had wide, black wings. None of them were shown in flight. Their eyes were large and appeared to glow, some red, some yellow, some green, out of the recesses of the vaulting.

"They are dead."

Snow-Eyes turned away from the fresco. The person who had spoken had walked up behind her unnoticed. Now, he giggled. A boy, not much older than Snow-Eyes, whose dark hair stuck out from the crown of his head, put his hands behind his back, glanced up at the ceiling and then shyly at her. "My mama told me those tekas died a long time ago. My name is Fern. What's yours."

"Snow-Eyes."

He giggled again and adjusted his sagging pants. "That's silly."

Hurt, she said, "I don't think it's silly."

"What's your mama's name?" He pointed to Edarra.

Snow-Eyes frowned. "Now you're being silly."

"Why? Doesn't she have a name? My mama's name is Ilonalla."

Snow-Eyes put her hands on her hips. "Yes, she has a name. But she's not a mama. Whatever is a mama?"

Fern laughed heartily. "Everybody's got one! That's mine, see?" He pointed to the dark woman with a shawl wrapped loosely around her shoulders, who was sitting next to Edarra on the bench. "She's talking to your mama."

"No, she's not! That's my sister."

Fern's eyes widened, and he scuffed one foot against his ankle. "She's a big sister. I don't have a sister."

"And I don't have a mama."

"But everybody . . ." The boy scratched his ear lobe. "Oh. I'm sorry. Did she go away to the Sea with the Lake Mother?"

Snow-Eyes glared at Fern. How did he know about the lady with the silver-eyes? Had Edarra somehow already given the painting to the Drake? She took a deep breath and bit her upper lip. No, she thought, Edarra couldn't've hidden the portrait from me in the coracle. Angry and scared, she was going to tell Fern she did not know what he was talking about, when Edarra called to her and she had to run off.

All the way home, Snow-Eyes puzzled over what the boy, Fern, had said. A couple of times she began to ask Edarra what a mama was and how Fern had known about the Lake Mother, but her sister's face was tight and unhappy-looking and forbade questions. She kept reprimanding Snow-Eyes for eating too much, too fast, or for moving when she had been told to sit still.

A few days after the sisters had returned from their journey, Snow-Eyes went to the front room and looked at the woman with the silver eyes. As she sat in the overstuffed chair, she decided that the painting must be a picture of her mama. She thought, If everybody has a mama, the Lake Mother must be mine.

The door to the room creaked open, and Paudan stuck his head in. "There you are, little one. Supper is ready." He opened the door wider and leaned against the carved drake on the center panel.

Snow-Eyes slipped down off the high-backed chair. "Paudan, is that lady my mama?" She nodded at the woman in the frame.

He walked into the room to glance up at the picture. He answered, "Yes and no."

She blinked. "What?" she said.

He sat down in the chair and put one arm around his daughter's waist. "That is a painting of the Lake Mother of Wyessa. She is no common Kieldean or fishwife, but a mama, as you called her, to all people in Woodmill. So you see, she is your mother—and mine as well, in a way. I have only seen her once—in a dream, many years ago. And so I painted her as I saw her, in my dream." He paused and gave his daughter a look of consideration. Then, he sighed. "She is also the sister of Death. Death lives in the Sea of Sansel's Net, on the other side of the world."

Snow-Eyes nodded gravely, recalling Fern's words.

Paudan continued, "Death is fearsome to many people—unforgiving as a snake and just as unpredictable. She turns the seasons round on a mighty pivot at the bottom of the sea, from winter to spring, spring to fall and back to winter. Yet, as terrible as she is, she is the one who keeps order in the world.

"Now, you mustn't think the Lake Mother is as fearsome as her sister, Death. No, no, the Lake Mother softens her sibling's nature. She brings rain when the sun is too harsh and melts the ice in winter. She gives flowers their fragrance and color and snowflakes their intricate beauty. She listens to the troubles we Kieldeans have—and also to our wishes. And when a person's time has come to go to Death's abode, the Lake Mother is their guide and comforter. See that green bowl on the table beneath the painting? I keep the bowl there so that I may give the Lake Mother each day a single, fresh-picked flower: a red sunstar bud in summer, a white snowstar bloom in winter. The floorcandle next to the table is for her, also. I keep it lit all night—see how the flame raises sparks of blue and rose-mauve off the guitar's mother-of-pearl? The mother-of-pearl is the Lake Mother's shell." He smiled.

Snow-Eyes asked, "But—do I have a ma—"

"We shall speak more of this some other time," said Paudan. "But our supper is getting cold, and Edarra will scold us both for tarrying."

☆

As Snow-Eyes grew older, she treasured the many tales that Paudan told of the Lake Mother. She would recount them in whispers to herself as she did her chores so that she would remember them, since none were written down in the books she was given to read. Her favorite tale was one that is told in Mossdon Kield to this day. They still tell it in the first language; it is about wild Aenan, the Tenebrian rider who became the Lake Mother's only consort and the father of her most precious child. And it told of how that poor child was taken away, taken away by jealous Death.

Sometimes when Snow-Eyes was alone, she would wander over to Lake Wyessa and stand on the shore to stare out at the island where the Lake Mother lived. On those days she would dream of Aenan and imagine she saw him swimming in the clear waters of the lake, looking for his lost child.

When she was alone at home, Snow-Eyes liked to sit in the front room to pose as still as the portrait posed, blinking languidly, as the portrait could not, and granting wishes to invisible suppliants. By the sign of a serious smile, which only the favored could interpret, she answered troubles and fulfilled dreams. Edan caught her at this game once. But he saw nothing unusual to his eyes, merely a child sitting as still as a tree in the dark.

When the summer came, Snow-Eyes preferred the atrium garden to the front room. There, she would lie in the grass beside the wishing stone. The stone was shiny, black and rounded. It was carved all over with vines and animals. Lambs slept along the stone's base and young bullocks stood above them; tiny frogs leapt across the bullocks' heads and one large owl embraced them all in its wings.

Snow-Eyes loved the owl in particular,

above the rest. It seemed solemn and wise and yet fierce, too. She told secrets to its wide eyes, and at night she would lie in bed and listen to its live brethren hooting to one another, talking in their owl language under the starry sky. Sometimes she thought she might like to be an owl herself, so that she could fly over the mountains to the sea, free and fierce and wise. Sometimes she used to feel sorry for the black stone owl, because it could not leave the garden, being stone.

"The wishing stones of Woodmill," said Paudan once, as he sat in the atrium with Snow-Eyes, "are gifts from the Lake Mother. When she had decided to leave her sister, Death, so that she might live among her Kieldeans, Death grew angry and rose up from the depths of the ocean. She hurled great rocks at her sister with a burning hand—so hot with anger was she that the stones themselves kindled. But the rocks did not touch the Lake Mother, and when they had cooled, she gathered them up and gave them to our ancestors. She told our grandmothers and grandfathers to sculpt her kindred's faces in the stone: the owl, who is her closest kindred, the frog, the lamb and the bullock. She promised that she would listen to any wishes made upon these stones." Paudan put his whittling knife down in the grass.

Snow-Eyes said, "If I make a wish now, will it come true?"

He rested his cheek on the back of his hand and said, "In the olden days, according to the Tales of Kheon, the Lake Mother used to leave her villa each seasonchange so that she could visit with her children's children, bless the wishing stones and answer wishes. But now the Lake Mother comes rarely, it seems, and most wishes wash over the stones like rain, sinking silent and unfulfilled into the earth. You might ask a wish she could or would answer. But be careful. Foolhardy wishes are soon regretted."

Snow-Eyes stared up at the summer sky. It was as clear as blue-glaze porcelain. Bees danced about the opened sunstars at her feet. Sitting next to Paudan with her back against the carved bullocks, she dreamt of all the wishes she might make, should the Lake Mother ever come a-blessing again. She glanced over at her father. He had picked up his whittling knife again and began to carve an untouched block of ebon wood.

She said, "Have you ever made a wish, Paudan?"

"Yes, little one."

"And did it come true?"

"Yes ..." He paused to brush his trousers clean of wood shavings. "Sometimes I wonder if I should not have made that wish at all." He shrugged. "Never mind, never mind. The wish was made a long time ago, and the Lake Mother shall not visit me or my dreams again, I daresay."

☆

Now it happened that one day when Snow-Eyes was ten winters old a visitor came. In the night, with the frost, the visitor came knocking so loudly on the front door that the sound woke the child, even though the bedroom she shared with Edarra was near the back of the house. She sat up and tucked her woollen blanket around her knees. As the knocking went on and on, she glanced over at Edarra. Her sister did not move. She pulled the blanket up around her shoulders, stared down at the convolvuli worked into the dark blue wool and she listened.

The knocking stopped. She heard the door open. A murmur of voices crept down the hall. She lay on her back and stared at the ceiling. Edarra turned over, rustling the straw ticking in her mattress.

Footsteps passed from the front hall to the front room. Snow-Eyes knew it to be the portrait's room because the door to it creaked: open, *tick*; shut, *tock*. She could not hear the murmuring voices anymore. Her sister snored and coughed. The wind whistled through the cracks of the thick-paned windows.

She could not fall back to sleep. She closed her eyes, but after a few moments found them open again, though the darkness was the same whether her eyes were open or shut. A window started to rattle. She began to hear strange scuttlings, as if the mice in the cellar had scampered up the stairs. Finally, she got down out of her warm bed to the icy floor. She was naked; the cold raised gooseflesh along her arms and dimpled her little brown nipples. She slipped a black shirt over her head, tugging it on. Tiptoeing past Edarra, she opened the door. She hoped that the hinges would not creak. They did not. After peering into the hall, where the air was even colder than the bedroom's, she stepped out.

In the garden atrium beyond the hall's columns, snow fell. Silently, silently it fell, drifting into the yard and covering over the bare earth. She leaned against one of the twisted granite columns and watched the garden whiten until she heard a muffled voice. Someone was singing. A moment later she heard the guitar accompanying the singer as gracefully as a bird might follow its mate in flight. This was strange. That guitar was never used. It stood in a corner of the front room. Though dusty and untouched, its mother-of-pearl inlays always gleamed, but it was never moved from the corner. Indeed, she had only heard the instrument played once, by Paudan. He had plucked the strings discordantly one afternoon when Snow-Eyes was very young. She remembered that he had been down at the lakeshore earlier that day.

Who is it; who is making Paudan play the guitar? she wondered. To whom would he play? She ran down the hallway's length, her bare feet slapping against the polished stone floor. She stopped at the front room's threshold, took a deep breath, made a wish that the half-opened door would not creak and pushed it. Her wish was granted.

She peeked in. The room was warm. A pyramid of small logs burned in the wide, blue-stone hearth and the fire's light shadowed the mantlepiece. Beneath the mantle, the stucco wall was tiled with glazed ceramics, which depicted scenes from the tales of the Alentine Islands, one tile from each major isle, one scene from each tale. Paudan sat next to the hearth with his back to the door, whittling. Beside him, on the edge of one of Edan's rugs, sat a woman dressed in a white shift, white trousers. She played the guitar, her head bent over the curve of the instrument and her waist-length hair tied back in a strand of itself. She sang. The words of the song went like this:

Oh, where have you gone,
my darkling child?
Have you followed the silvern
down to the sea?
I have gone nowhere,
O my mother.
I have not followed the silvern
nor followed the sea . . .

Paudan murmured, "Shall I sing with you, as we once did?"

The young woman laughed. "I wish it —please."

Firelight flashed off the mother-of-pearl inlays, off Paudan's knife and off the dangling mirrors the visitor wore as earrings. Neither the father nor the stranger noticed Snow-Eyes peeking in at them. She craned her neck to see the picture of the Lake Mother on the wall and compare it to the stranger's face. But the sheen of the paint's varnish hid the image's features.

Paudan put down his whittling and stood. He placed his hand on the stranger's shoulder and caressed her hair. Snow-Eyes stepped back and pulled the door shut, swift and silent. Who was that woman? The child ran down the hall, hooked a column in the crook of her arm and stopped at the edge of the garden. She was shivering. Her heart pounded.

He loves her . . . she thought as she glanced over her shoulder at the door of the front room. She must be the Lake Mother—who else? She's come! Will we have a wish? Has she blessed our wishing stone . . . will she?

Snow-Eyes looked into the garden. Heavy, fat flakes of snow were still falling onto the browned grass and into the empty flowerbeds. A ring of white circled the base of stone where ivy usually grew. A small mound of snow capped the owl. The child dared herself to walk out to it.

"Go," she whispered at her legs. "Go."

She stepped onto the path. The cold burned her naked feet, but she pushed on across the garden to the owl's side. If it had been blessed, it did not look any different to her. She brushed off the snow powder. Fitting her numbed toes in between the carved lambs and on top of the bullocks' heads, she climbed onto the owl's back and stared up at the sky. There was no moon. There were no stars. She stuck out her tongue to catch the flakes and pretended that they were sweet, as sweet as sugar from the clouds should be.

"There she is, Paudan."

Snow-Eyes gave a start at the sound of the stranger's voice, and she slipped a little. Clutching the stone owl's beak so that she would not fall, she turned around. Paudan and the visitor stood between two twisted columns. The child climbed down off her perch and started walking up the path toward them. The snow melted in her straight, dark hair.

Paudan made a sound in the back of his throat. She thought for a moment that he was going to pretend he was a bear, as he did sometimes in jest. But he was not playing now. He strode into the garden, crunching the ice underfoot, and he said, "My little one, you are turning blue! What are you doing out of bed?" He picked her up and held her on one hip so that he could chafe warmth into her bare legs.

Before she could answer her father, the stranger laughed. The mirror earrings that she wore jingled as the young woman walked. She put her long hand on top of the wishing stone.

Snow-Eyes wanted to touch the woman's earrings and try them in her own ears, which Edarra had lately pierced and strung with thread. She was surprised, and disappointed, to see that although the stranger had the same silver-white eyes as the Lake Mother's picture did, she did not have the same face. And yet, despite her disappointment, the child thought that she had never seen anyone so handsome before, not even Edan, who had dark-lashed auburn eyes; not even Edarra, whose skin was as soft as fleece. She wanted to ask the woman, "How did you learn to play the guitar? Where did your earrings come from? What is your name? Are you the Lake Mother?" But she was too shy. She clutched at her father's shirt and stared at the visitor.

The woman stroked the owl's smooth head. "What is your name, child?" she asked.

Snow-Eyes said, "Which name?"

"Do you have more than one?"

"Oh, yes. My Kielding name is Amarra Nie. But I have another—it's Snow-Eyes."

The woman glanced at Paudan and said sharply, "Why do you call her this?"

"After you—your eyes . . ." he answered. "Of course, after you." His voice quivered; there was a tone of uncertainty in it that Snow-Eyes had never heard before. She looked at her father's face some long moments. There were sad lines around his mouth and eyes.

What is wrong? she wondered. Why is his voice so sad? She let go of his shirt collar and turned to stare at the stranger, whose gaze seemed harder than silver, more chill than the ice on the black stone. The child leaned away from her father suddenly, pointed her tiny finger at the woman and said, "Go home. Go away!"

The visitor frowned and stepped back. Then she caught her breath, turned and bent her head.

Paudan put his daughter down. "What is it, Beya? The little one didn't mean—"

"What?" cried Snow-Eyes. "What did I do?"

No one answered her. The woman did not look around, and Paudan stood silently by her side with his hand on her shoulder.

"What did I do?" Snow-Eyes ran after her father and hugged his waist. "Paudan, Paudan, I didn't do anything! She was mean to you, and she doesn't like my name . . ."

"No, no, come here." He knelt to the frantic child and pressed his cheek to her chest. "You didn't do anything," he whispered.

She wrapped her arms around his neck. He smelled of woodsmoke and wet wool and of himself. She slid her hands inside his shirt collar to warm them and asked him to carry her back to bed. He lifted her off the ground.

"She's strong, even now," said the stranger. "A strong will."

Paudan answered hesitantly, "She's very bright . . . I . . . I've been teaching her, as you wished."

"And what have you taught her?"

Snow-Eyes looked up from her father's shoulder and said, "I can talk for myself."

The woman laughed. "Can you now?" she said. Her clear eyes had a sheen to them; they glistened like the polished mirrors she wore in her ears. "Tell me, what have you learned?"

"A lot." Snow-Eyes shivered and yawned. "I want to go to bed."

Paudan nodded and rocked her in his arms. He said, "She's tired, Beya. You can talk to her in the morning."

"No, I can't. I'm not staying the night."

"You aren't? But—"

"I know, I know . . . I'll come back, when I can."

He started to speak, then did not.

Snow-Eyes laid her head down against the curve of Paudan's neck and closed her eyes. She drifted into sleep, dreaming of herself riding a bullock bareback. The murmur of the stranger's voice turned into the murmur of the sea, where she rode in the sand on the bullock, slowly . . .

Paudan said loudly, "You're not coming back to me, are you? Not now, not ever."

"I will—oh, Paudan, I try to visit more . . . but I can't— "

Snow-Eyes woke and opened her eyes to the woman's dark face.

"Amarra?" said the stranger.

"I want to go to bed."

"In a moment. Tell me, what is this, here?"

The child looked down, pushing away the sea-dream. She saw that the woman with the frost in her eyes was touching the owl's head with one finger, so she answered, "Our wishing stone." Rubbing her face, she shook off her sleepiness.

"And do you ever wish upon it?"

"Sometimes." The child glanced at her father. "I don't wish for foolish things. I promise. I don't."

Paudan smiled. The sad lines on his face smoothed.

The young woman stepped away from the carved stone. "Come and make a wish."

"Beya—" said Paudan.

"Only one." She nodded. The mirror earrings jingled. "It's a special night. So, child, think very hard and wish very quietly and then we shall take you to bed."

Snow-Eyes stammered, "Are . . . a-are you the Lake Mother?"

"My name is Beya Rete. Here now—" She tapped the stone.

Wriggling until her father was forced to let her go, she walked up the path. Pushing back the wet hair that clung like black feathers to her cheeks, she clambered atop the owl's back again to make a wish, as she had been taught. Everything that she had ever dreamt of crowded in her head, and she did not know which of them to choose. Afraid lest she take too much time, she closed her eyes and wished, without speaking, three of the things she most wanted: that she would not be such a little child anymore, that her brother and sister would not scold or tease her and . . . she peeked at the woman called Beya . . . to be like the Lake Mother someday, to have silver earrings and make wishes true. To be strong.

When her wish was done, she was even more tired than before. Wearily she climbed off the stone and knelt before it, putting her hands over the owls's eyes. At last she stood, her knees angry red from the cold, and she patted her waist, shoulders, chest—had she not grown?

No. She stared up at the woman. She waited to grow. But nothing happened. She said, "Won't you make my wishes true?"

"They are true," said Beya softly. "In time."

The child's lower lip quivered. "No, they aren't. You're not the Lake Mother. You lied!"

"I told you my name."

"No!"

Paudan hastily picked up his daughter and said, "Hush, hush, now." This time, he took her off to bed. As he shut the bedroom door, he whispered to the stranger, "What did she ask for?"

Snow-Eyes raised her head, listening.

"You know I can't tell you," said Beya. "No, Paudan."

There was a pause. Snow-Eyes sat up.

Paudan said, "I don't want her to go with you."

"Not now. In a year ..."

"Never. I don't want her to suffer, as you and I have suffered."

There was another, longer pause. The silence made Snow-Eyes want to go to the door. Did they leave? she wondered. She tried to see her father through the crack between the door and its frame. But there was only darkness.

The woman said, "She is my child."

"And mine." Paudan raised his voice. "If you won't stay to share her childhood with me, then—"

"I can't!"

"But why? Why?"

"I—can't."

"Beya—"

"Listen to me, Paudan. Our daughter has the gift. Sooner or later, she will want to use her gift. She will ask you questions that you can't answer, she will see things you can't see. She will need me, then, and I will return for her."

"No."

"Come—come away from here. We shall wake them both, arguing."

The door was closed and silence took over the room.

Snow-Eyes stared at the ceiling, lying back down in bed. She was bone cold. Mother? she thought and then shook her head. My mother? Shivering again, she held onto her blanket with two, tight fists. I won't go anywhere with that lady. Not even if she begs. Paudan won't let her take me away! I won't go—I don't want—I'll unwish my wishes right now. She closed her eyes, pictured the the stone owl and whispered into her pillow that she wanted to be only herself, only Snow-Eyes.

But a voice seemed to speak in her ear. It said, "She's my child."

"No!" she murmured fiercely. Rocking herself with her legs tucked up against her stomach, she told herself that the stranger could not have been the Lake Mother, no, no, not at all. The Lake Mother would not have lied. The Lake Mother would have granted the wishes.

And, thought the child as she pulled up the blanket so that it covered her head, if she were really my own, true mama, as she said she was, then she wouldn't have made Paudan so unhappy. She was lying, she must have been lying. Snow-Eyes clutched her pillow and whispered to herself that she had been having a nightmare, a nightmare, and when she woke up it would all be gone, just as fast as the snow would melt when the sun shone at the dawn. Willing herself to believe the woman with the silver eyes a nightmare, wishing to forget what she had heard the woman say, the girl slept.

2

The Bells

THE NEXT morning, Snow-Eyes refused to speak to Paudan about the midnight visitor, and as time went on, the silver-eyed woman was banished from her memory, as she had wished. All that remained of the woman was a feeling, undefined, like the shadow of a nightmare. Snow-Eyes forgot the unfulfilled wishes and the words whispered outside her door and the sound of the guitar's strings softly strummed. Paudan did not question her again, and the days passed as they had passed always, except that she avoided the wishing stone altogether. If she happened by the carved owl's face at night, a cold dread made her hurry away, though she could not have said why.

And as she grew older, she began to understand how poor her family had become. Two seasons of bad harvests and Paudan's dwindling skills caused hardship; worst of all, it broke Paudan's heart to see his chil-

dren in need. The roof of the villa leaked in
the kitchen during the spring's rain; the
meals, which had once seemed filling, were
scant. The nut porridge Snow-Eyes ate on
early winter mornings was often too thin to
carry her through midday. There were nights
and nights when supper was simply boiled
cabbage and potatoes.

Summer was a better time for the Nies.
Vegetables from the land filled their table.
Occasionally they had meat from an eggless
hen or an unwary snake. The days were
warm, and the woods blossomed with wild
berries and tree nuts and the lake ran with
fish; the garden bloomed. But even so, most
of the peas, wax beans, squash and cabbage
went to the Drake Villae's table. Snow-Eyes
had come to know that on her long-ago
visit to Woodmill, the Drake had refused
the portrait as a gift, being uninterested in
another likeness of the Lake Mother—she
had been given several over the years and
through she had once admired Paudan Nie's
work, her tastes had changed and she had
forgotten his portrait. The next season, the
tax of the valley people had become greater
and that, along with the poor harvests the
Nies suffered, made things very hard indeed.

The burden of poverty aged Paudan. He
had led a wandering life and had never
thought to save, and now he felt powerless.
Snow-Eyes watched old age take him swiftly.

At the outset of each year, he would have his youngest child stand against his workroom's lintel and he would mark her new height on the jamb in red chalk. As he did this, muttering all the while that she had not, by the Mother's granting, inherited the cursed height of the Nie family, she would examine him in turn. And so she had seen the wrinkles zigzag the sad lines around his eyes, and she had watched the red hair on the backs of his hands turn white. His hands stiffened year by year so that he had to hold the marking chalk awkwardly with thumb and third finger.

She knew also that soon he would be unable to practice his carpentry at all. As it was, he already spent most of his time alone in his workroom, surrounded by unfinished animal figurines. He sat and smoked the pipe he had carved for himself—a pipe of blanched oak, shaped like a bear.

Since Edan farmed and Edarra was seldom home, it fell to Snow-Eyes to care for her father, as he had once cared for her. She made his meals. She fed coals to the green copper brazier in his workroom. In the evening, she would sit with him and listen to any story he might wish to tell.

"I was born," he said to her, "in a seaside villa, at the border of Kield Woodmill and the lands of Kheon Kield. As a boy, I learned to fish and to sail and I learned how to fashion sturdy boats—wherries and cora-cles—for the fishers.

"One day a sunburnt sailor came to my villa. My brothers had found her on the beach. She was ill from exposure. Her boat and its crew had been lost in a storm. We nursed her, my brothers and I, and we listened to her tales eagerly. As she healed, she asked us if we could build her a ketch, and then, when the boat was done, she asked us if we would crew for her. On that day I found that I had a traveler's heart. I left home with the sailor. She was my first love, Eda Wellen, and we went off on the back of the White Sea together to see wondrous sights and to find the meaning of all things. I read answers, or so I thought, in the stars as I stood beside the ketch's mizzenmast, astrolabe in one hand, supper in the other.

"Time passed. The wonder I had thought to see, I never found—it was always one island away, always on the next shore. Instead, I found sickness and the dark, decaying Kields of other lands, and finally, an unending desire to find my way home again. In my heart I remembered the Lake Mother of Wyessa and I wished to her. I wished that she might help me find my home again. I dreamt of her.

"But time passed. Eda led us hither and thither over the White Sea. She was searching, she said, for the mendiri."

"What is that?" asked Snow-Eyes.

"They are fabled creatures, come from the mountains of the northwest, and they have the secret of life eternal. The tales say that the secret is so terrible that there are only two mendiri in all the world now—and some tellers have said that these two killed themselves long ago because the weight of life everlasting was too great. In the beginning, I wanted to find the mendiri as much as my Eda did. I wanted to wrest the secret from them. But soon all I really wanted was a home. For a little while, we lived on the Alentine Island called Kyrilt, where Eda had been born. Her father gave me a new name—Paudan—which I was proud to accept. It means, 'child of my heart.'

"Finally, Eda and I set sail again. Slowly, I drew her back to Gueame and here, to Woodmill. We found this villa. And time passed. Edan and Edarra were born. Whatever became of the mendiri we never did discover, nor did we hear more of them, except perhaps in the sadness of a storm's wind.

"Then, before little Edan could even walk, his mother caught a winter fever. At that spring's last blossoming, Eda left us. The Lake Mother came for her the very day that spring turned to summer, the very day the bells of seasonchange rang. The Lake Mother came to take Eda away and to guide her to the Sea." He stopped speaking and lit his pipe.

Snow-Eyes waited until the tobacco shag caught the flame. Then she said, "What about me?"

He smiled absently, staring at a tiny puff of smoke. "You are a spring blossom, little one; a gift of seasonchange."

"I don't understand. Eda was not my mother—I am too little, too young."

"I just told you—you were a gift."

She laughed and shook her head. "No, Paudan, you can't make me believe that you found me in the heart of a sunstar. Who was my mother?"

Taking the pipe stem from his mouth, he glanced at his daughter. "You don't remember."

"No. How should I? Did she not go away when I was a baby?"

He nodded. "So you were. And I think that it is better you don't remember."

Pressed for an answer by his daughter, Paudan remained stubbornly mute. Unsatisfied and a little scared by his silence, Snow-Eyes went off to pester Edan and Edarra.

But they, too, grew silent at her questioning. Finally, Edarra said, "Your mother was a strange, beautiful lady; dark haired, tall and very quiet." Edarra laughed softly. "Sometimes I used to think she was the Lake Mother, because she was so beautiful and because Paudan painted that portrait to resemble her, a little. but I don't remember a lot about her, because she never paid us—Edan and I—much mind."

Edan shook his head. "She was always going away, even while she was carrying you. And then, after you were born, she went away one day and never came home again."

"We waited," said Edarra. "Paudan is still waiting, though he will not speak of her anymore." The older girl put her hand on Snow-Eyes's shoulder. "I'm sorry, little one. She went away and won't come back. It is best to forget—you have Paudan, and I am here and Edan. We are your family, and we love you."

Snow-Eyes felt her heart close up like a morning glory at noon. But she nodded and nothing else was said, and after a while she left her brother and sister to go off by herself and ponder what she had heard.

For a long time after that, Snow-Eyes tried to recall something, anything about her mother—a smile or a scent or the touch of a hand. But each time she tried, a terrible feeling came over her, like the chill of snow and icy winds. A whisper of music seemed to sound inside her head and it carried a mood of darkness, a darkness that dulled the beauty of the flowers in her garden and challenged her to find any joy at all in her days. So, as she got older, she ceased asking either herself or her brother and sister. She decided that her mother must have done something awful—why else would she have left? Unless she had not wanted her new little baby. Making up her mind that one or the other must be true, Snow-Eyes kept the secret of her mother's disgrace to herself. Whatever the disgrace was, Snow-Eyes was afraid that if her brother or sister guessed it, they might go away too.

As the girl became stronger and older, she began to take on larger and larger tasks; she helped her brother plant in the spring; she watched the sheep on the hills in summer; she wove their wool into cloth in the fall and took care of Paudan all the while. Her little hands grew long and calloused. She became thin and hard-muscled from working.

She seldom went far, though she thought about other lands. She tried to imagine the Alentine Islands and dreamt about traveling as free as her father had once been. Then, in the summer of her first blood-flow, Edarra took Snow-Eyes down to the sea. The journey was a Kyriltian custom, to honor the new-made woman. It was a journey that Edarra's mother had once promised her, but had not lived to fulfill.

Snow-Eyes could not contain her joy. It would be the first time she had left home

since her visit to Kield Woodmill. It would
be the first time she would see the White
Sea, though she had been told about it by
Paudan and had read of it in his books.

On the morning after her bleeding began,
she and Edarra left the villa before sunrise,
paddling their coracle across Lake Wyessa
down to the flat Middlemost. Four sunrises
took them to the river's mouth. There they
towed the coracle to the rocky bank and
hiked across the reddish blade lancets onto
the sand and past humped dunes. Walking
between hummocks of scanty grass, they
came to a wide stretch of land under an
empty stretch of sky. Both sky and sand
were met and mingled by the wide, sharding
shimmer of the sea. The wind tore at their
clothes. The rushing water frothed and
spread a crystal sheet on the sand. Splin-
tered, softened gray logs, twice the size of a
child, and twigs, thinner than a blue crown's
leg, were heaped in tangles, marking out a
barricade where bladed earth abutted dry,
peppery sand. Barren cliffs bordered the expanse on either side of the cove. Snow-Eyes
watched gray sea gillians skim the water's
surface, dive, skim, dive and disappear, the
echoes of their cries sounding horrible and
human. The girl timidly followed her older
sister to the sea's edge.

Staring at the hurtling waves, she wanted
to shout. The sea filled and took her over, it

seemed, took over everything: land, sky, child's heart, soul, all, given over in that instant. The backs of her knees felt wet with a cold sweat. Her feet and hands felt as if they had dropped off. She sat down. Under the heels of her black sheepskin boots, the sand was churned, unearthing several tiny spear shells. Vermicular and crimson, the shells looked like the blooded daggers of sand imps, or the lost teeth of an infant sea dragon.

The older girl sat down beside her sister and put her arm around Snow-Eyes, who then rested her head against Edarra's shoulder. Without speaking, they shared each other's warmth and watched the dying light of the huge, flaming summer sun.

Edarra was the first to stir. She said, "We shall need to make a fire. For the night. It is getting cold already. And dark."

Snow-Eyes leaned forward and picked out one of the spear shells from under her feet. She shook granules of sand from it to find it abandoned by its maker's death—a perfect and empty creation. She said, "I'd like to walk in the sea first, as the custom you told me about asks."

"Soon. A fire—"

"But," said Snow-Eyes, dismayed, "the sun is setting. Shouldn't I walk before—"

Edarra held her hand out with her fingers fisted and her thumb extended. "The

sun will set soon. We shall need a fire before it does. Help me gather the wood."

"There's plenty, all around us. We'll find
enough, even if it is dark."

"No. It's cold." Edarra stood up.

"But the custom! You said I had to walk
in the sea while the sun set. Let me go now,
before—"

"No."

Snow-Eyes stood also and touched her
sister's shoulder. "Why? What is wrong?"

Edarra pulled away from her sister
roughly. Surprised, Snow-Eyes lost her balance and staggered a bit. The spear shell
she had picked up was knocked from her
hand. It spun into the blade behind them
and was lost.

Snow-Eyes stared after the shell. "I don't
understand. Why?"

Edarra did not turn around. "Because,"
she said tightly, "I will not be without a
fire, when the dark comes."

"You won't be. I'm going to walk."

Edarra grabbed her sister's arm. "Please—
you can do the walking tomorrow's eve."

"It's my blooding—what if there is no
blood, tomorrow?" She shook off Edarra's
hand and ran down to the water. The sun
hung a thumb's width above the sea and
was masked, in part, by a line of violet
clouds. Snow-Eyes stood rigid, arms folded
and teeth clenched, letting her boot soles be

christened with foam before she took off her black shirt, black trousers, boots and all. She bit her upper lip as she untied the laces, thinking, What is wrong with Edarra? Can't she see that I must walk now?

The water was cold. At first her ankles ached with it and her knees ached and she lost sensation in her thighs. The sea's rush to the shore staggered her backward; its sand-scouring retreat tugged her forward. She walked in it with respect for the power that let her dally there, like a giant might let a butterfly dance upon its fingertips. She laughed, and arching her back, she did a dance. In and out of the giant's fingers she ran and leapt, her broad face laced with salt and sea spray.

But she did not remain long in the ocean, mindful that her blood might draw the sea dragon's dark, rapacious brother, named shark. She was aware, too, that the sun had now vanished under the water. She began to feel remorseful about her sister. Something was bothering Edarra, something about the darkness and the cold. Snow-Eyes gathered up her clothes and walked back to where Edarra had set a small fire going, sheltered between two massive logs. As the younger sister sat near the blaze, dripping water onto the sand as if her whole body was crying salt tears, Edarra looked up and said, "You aren't afraid."

"Of what?"

"The dark." Edarra regarded her sister almost as if she had never seen Snow-Eyes before.

The young girl hugged her knees. She looked into the tiny fire. "I am afraid of darkness. But not the dark of the eve, or of the night sky."

"What other sort of darkness is there? You were at the sea's edge, dancing. I saw. You weren't afraid at all."

"I could see your fire."

"You weren't afraid."

"Yes, I am," said Snow-Eyes vehemently. "Of the dark that comes when I'm lonely, of the dark that comes when I feel that everyone else has gone away and I am the only one left in the whole wide world."

Edarra stared. Snow-Eyes could see that her sister did not believe her or did not understand. This made her feel so alone and different that she was suddenly afraid and she shivered.

For the rest of the evening, the two girls spoke of little things or not at all. They ate in silence and spread their blankets in silence and crawled in between them without words. Snow-Eyes curled her toes against the warmed, wrapped rock at the bottom of her bedding and stared at the clear, starred sky. Her heart was pounding, louder to her ears than the distant surf. She could not sleep. She told herself, as if she were talking to Edarra, "See? There's no darkness here—look, look at the night, shot through with stars! And the blue moon there, see it? It's light, blue and light. And I have touched the White Sea with my blood, and the sea has touched me."

Sighing, Snow-Eyes turned over onto her stomach, breathing slowly. She tried to brush the sand off her wind-chapped face, but there were so many tiny, sharp grains clinging to her eyelids, nose and chin that she stopped trying. She peered over at her sister. Edarra had fallen asleep already. Her braided hair was a deep red in the dying fire's light. Her face was peaceful.

Snow-Eyes put her head in her arms and whispered, "I am not alone." Her heart pounded; she could feel the beat of her blood at the base of her neck.

A moment later, or so it seemed, Edarra sat up, dragging most of the blanket with her. The rush of chilly wind woke Snow-Eyes. She grabbed the edge of the covers, tugged on them and then sat up too. The fire spat cinders like rain. The breeze grew stronger.

"What is it?" whispered Snow-Eyes.

Edarra did not answer. The surf grumbled in the distance and the fire spat again, but the wind had died as suddenly as it had come.

Quiet.

The girl heard nothing odd. She saw nothing but—

Eyes.

Round and slanting, almond and pebble, four pairs of disembodied eyes, all of them as bright as stars come down to earth. They watched her.

Snow-Eyes felt cold fear empty her of all will. She sat with her hands clenched against her stomach, breathing too fast and becoming lightheaded.

Beyond the ring of the fire's warmth, yet reflecting its light, the blinking eyes seemed to be everywhere, moving about her and giving the darkness itself sight. The eyes were nearly blue, but not quite—they were made of something colder than blue, more adamantine than ice. They flashed. And as they watched her, Snow-Eyes thought she could see the faces to which the eyes belonged. Four long faces. Women's faces.

"Edarra ..." whispered the girl. "Edarra?" She was shuddering now, trying to fight off nausea. But whichever way she turned, so turned the eyes.

"Who are you?" she cried out, but her voice did not carry far. She did not expect an answer, not really. She did not get one.

She closed her eyes and muttered, "Oh, go away, whatever you are!" She huddled against her sister's warm back, her breasts

58

pressed to the other's spine, her face pressed to the other's shoulder. She hoped Edarra would wake and comfort her, if she clung to her this way, but when the older girl did not stir, Snow-Eyes willed herself to ignore the eyes and call them a nightmare. She narrowed her vision so that she might see only the freckles on her sister's neck. She tried to sleep.

☆

"Get up, get off me—"

Snow-Eyes woke to her sister's plea at first light. She moved, and Edarra rolled to her feet. The elder girl brushed sand from her shoulders and rubbed her neck.

Snow-Eyes scrambled out of the blankets and looked around her. A thin dawn light suffused the sand and touched the blade lancets with its pure gold. The empty beach spread out before her. The air was cool and fresh.

She and Edarra were alone. "They're gone!" she said and was so relieved that she sat back down and smiled.

"Who's gone?"

"Those creatures . . . those women, watching us last night. The eyes! You saw them."

"Eyes? You don't mean the stars, do you? They aren't eyes, little one!"

"No, no. All around us, last night. You

saw up and pointed to them and when I looked I saw their faces—"

"I did not sit up." Edarra stirred the embers of the evening's fire, seeking flame. She blew on the white ash and charred wood. A coal glowed dully. Edarra said, "I slept through the night. I did not sit up. I did not point at anything."

"You did, I—"

"No. You must've dreamt that I did. You must have been dreaming about these eyes and these women." Edarra stood, abruptly ending the argument, and she walked toward the banks of the Middlemost. Snow-Eyes hesitated briefly. Edarra had called her a liar. She felt her cheeks redden. Then she got up and went after her sister. The two girls washed the sand and the salt from themselves.

After eating, they went down to the sea's edge. Kyriltian custom demanded that a new-made woman not only walk in the sea at night's birth, but also that she drink a draught of sea-water at sun's height. Snow-Eyes and Edarra walked along as the sun climbed in a cloudless sky. Edarra carried two cups.

"You didn't see anything last night?" Snow-Eyes ventured to ask. "You never woke or sat up?"

"No . . . I . . . not that I remember. No." Edarra looked out over the high cresting waves. "What else did you dream? Tell me—what did you dream besides these eyes and these women? What did they do?"

"I'm not sure what else I dreamt. They were watching us. Perhaps it was a nightmare, as you say."

"Oh, surely. Surely it was. You can't think there was anyone besides ourselves on the beach last night! If there had been, why did they not speak to us? And you called them creatures first, not women. What sort of creatures?"

But Snow-Eyes did not answer. After a while, she shrugged. "I think it might have been only an owl. Being half-awake, I made the owl many-eyed and fearsome."

"Oh." Edarra squinted at the sun and crouched to fill the two cups. "Here." The sisters tasted the sea.

Edarra smiled. "Paudan told me to say to you, 'Now you are a woman, now you are beginning the way to who you are. Be thou quick and be thou careful.'" The elder sister hugged Snow-Eyes. "That's what the women say to one another on Kyrilt. Come here, little one." She kissed Snow-Eyes on both cheeks.

☆

During the journey home, neither sister mentioned the creatures in Snow-Eyes' dream.

They spoke instead of motherhood and of children and of perhaps visiting Woodmill Kield more often, to search out the company of men. But while Snow-Eyes spoke about all these concerns, in her heart she pondered her dream. She knew that she had not been asleep and that she had not been dreaming—at least not the sort of dreaming to which she was accustomed, the kind that sleep fostered. No, no, she had seen strange and watching eyes of some strange and watching women, who had stolen upon the sisters in the darkness and had gone away by morning. Snow-Eyes thought they must be very like creatures of the night, to be so swift and noiseless. But she felt sure that they had been women, and she knew that they had been standing there, making footprints in the sand.

Summer passed to winter and winter into spring and the Nies grew poorer still. Snow-Eyes worked hard in the fields beside Edan but the harvests continued to be smaller than they hoped for. And she found that although her body had become a woman's, she was still the littlest one to her family. No matter how old she grew, nor how many seasons flew by, she would always seem the child to her brother and sister and father. She took to keeping apart from them and, even though she had been given a choice, she still dressed herself in the black that

Paudan had chosen for her long ago. The simple, dark garments set her apart from Edan and Edarra, made her different from them. Sometimes Edan called her sullen for this and sometimes silly, but she kept to the black anyway.

One spring morning, after she had risen from bed and was walking around the hall that bordered the garden, she passed Paudan's workroom to find him up already and dressed. He stood beside the open window. Smoke drifted from his pipe out into the cool, spring air. She stepped across the threshold, meaning to ask him why he was awake so early, when she heard a bell ringing. The bell's tone was high, gentle and faint. It seemed to wander across the green cornfield on the back of a honeysuckle-sweet breeze. She sidled closer to the window.

It was the Lake Mother's bell, bespeaking the advent of a new season. The sweet breeze ruffled the girl's hair, and the flower-scent mingled with the bitter shag smoke of Paudan's pipe. Two bells rang, then three, now four, a carillon sounding loud, soft, loud, soft, at the wind's whim.

Snow-Eyes listened closely. There was something odd about the sound . . . the bells were turning into voices. Singing. The words of the song, through faint, were clear to her—and she thought she had heard the song before.

I have gone nowhere,
O my mother.
I have not followed the silvern
nor followed the sea . . .
My eyes cannot see you,
my darkling child.
You have fled from my side,
oh, where can you be?

The tune reminded Snow-Eyes of something or someone. She frowned, trying to catch the memory as it slid away like the sly silvern in the song. She grasped the windowsill and leaned out, straining to hear more of the words. But the light voices had become bell tones again, and then they seemed to be calling to her . . . Amarra . . . Amarra . . . Amarra . . .

Paudan said, "Snow-Eyes?"

The voices quieted. The bells rang softer, no longer calling.

"Snow-Eyes?"

She turned to him. In one of his crooked, misshapen hands he held his pipe. Ash, unseen to him, spilled on the floor. With his other hand, he touched her elbow.

She ran her hand through her hair and asked, "Where were those voices coming from?"

"Voices?"

"A song. Singing. I heard—"

"You heard the bells of seasonchange."

"Yes, but I also heard singing . . ."

He shook his head and looked to the floor. A small tuft of fallen ash had gathered at his feet. He said, "The same bells ring each seasonchange. You know that."

She glanced out the window at the corn tassels shivering in the wind. The honey-suckle-scent tasted stronger. The sun warmed the night-cooled land. "I know I have heard that song before. but I can't remember . . ."

Paudan laughed and brushed a strand of his daughter's long hair behind her ear. "There was no song, little one. Just the bells."

"But—"

"Edarra tells me that you saw animals at the sea's edge when there were no animals. Isn't this true? You were dreaming then, on the beach. You are daydreaming now. There were no voices. I am telling you." He rapped his knuckles on the windowsill for emphasis and looked at her sternly.

Snow-Eyes hid her face from him and stared at the field beneath the heat-shrouded blue-green hills beyond their land. She had believed that Edarra had forgotten about the beach dream—or not-dream, as Snow-Eyes had called it. Because of Edarra's dismissal, the girl had not spoken about all the other not-dreams she had had since the day of her blooding ceremony. She never mentioned to anyone all the glimpses she had caught of strange things in the shadows and of the half-formed figures that no one else remarked upon. Only yesterday she had touched the little wooden animals in Paudan's workroom and had seen them each come alive for an instant, dancing at her fingertips, their incised fur or feathers feeling warm and silky against her skin. She had not told of these things because they were not dreams and yet she sensed that Edan and Edarra would have chided her for dreaming, just as Paudan was now.

There had been voices in the bells of seasonchange.

She said, "The bells—"

"Of course you heard those—so did I." Paudan placed his pipe stem in his mouth and breathed in, making the bear's open back glow. Letting out minute puffs of smoke, one at a time, he said, "I woke early and thought I would help make the breakfast."

She nodded. Yet even as she followed Paudan down the hall to the kitchen, she could almost hear the bellsong's strange, familiar patterning again. She puzzled over the words.

As father and daughter walked past the twisted columns, Snow-Eyes glanced into the garden, where the last spring flowers had opened their white and purple hearts to the sun. The wishing stone glistened, wet with dew. It was hugged around by the wide, waxy leaves of the ivy. The stone owl seemed to peer at her blindly.

And it flapped its great, sable wings.

She hurried after her father, stumbling across the kitchen's step. Would the owl follow her? She waited, afraid. She could not take her gaze from the doorway.

Silence.

Finally, she began to slit open chestnuts one by one, telling herself that she had been mistaken. The owl had not moved. Stone could not move. She stole a glance at the kitchen door.

Could stone move?

No.

She had no name for all these untrue things that were happening to her, other than not-dream, but as she ground up the nut meats for the porridge, she decided that despite what Paudan had said, she had heard singing in the bells. She looked over at him from under the cover of her dark bangs. He sat by the hearth with a steaming mug, his back to her. Stubbornly she thought at his shoulders, I did not daydream the song, paudan. And the voices of the bells were calling my name.

3

Paudan

THAT SUMMER brought hot, dry days to Kield Woodmill. Locusts whined in the bamboo groves and the earth became dry and parched, cracking in great dun flakes and filling the air with dust when the wind blew. Edan and Snow-Eyes hauled bucket after bucket of water up from Lake Wyessa, trying to keep what crops they could alive. But the corn stalks browned and the corn kernels shriveled; the cabbages were small and ragged. Edan's face was puckered with worry and his skin reddened and wrinkled from the sun. Edarra came home from her usual summer travels to help. The heat went on.

Even as the summer cooled, dying into autumn, the sky remained clear; cloudless and rainless. Sheep perished of thirst. People from the farthest reaches of the Kielding came to the lake for water as the Middlemost and its tributaries dwindled down to thin, muddy trickles. Many a wish was made, but the Lake Mother did not bring the rain.

Paudan became ill. At first, he suffered only a slight fever, and he nursed himself without telling his children about it because he deemed that they had enough to worry over. But the fever worsened, and in the midsummer's heat became unbearable to him. He withered to half his weight. Even lying utterly still in bed, he soaked the bedclothes with his sweat.

A sadness filled the shadowed halls, and a grim sort of patience walked with Edan and Edarra as they went about their work. Snow-Eyes did not quite understand their sorrow, but it frightened her; and at night, in the darkness of her own bed, she would lie awake and neither sleep nor dream.

The heat continued. Edan grew more silent and withdrawn with each day that passed. Finally, he said that he could not bear to lose both his father and his home when the winter arrived and the tithing came due, and so he had decided to visit Woodmill Kield. He had made up his mind to ask the advice of a healer for Paudan and to humbly beg the Drake Villae to reduce the season's tithe.

Snow-Eyes accompanied him only to the shores of Lake Wyessa, even though she wished to go with him to the Kield. Along the way, she tried to lighten his spirits a little by singing songs he had taught her. Walking through the bamboo thicket near the lake, carrying his satchel and his lunch, she sang a song for him about a star that fell to earth and became a shining bird. Every now and then he would murmur a few of the words with her, but then he would stop.

She faltered when he dropped the song for the third time. "Must you go?" she said. "Must you go alone?"

He pushed aside a branch, and she ducked underneath. He said, "I don't know what else to do. Paudan needs nursing and someone must tend the fields. I must go alone."

"He might get better."

"Not likely. Not without a healer." He closed his eyes for a moment. "I've seen this fever once before. My mother . . . I wish . . ."

"I do too," she said. "I wish he weren't so ill."

They headed down past brambled berry bushes and through the seeding grass. The lake shimmered. He walked over to a cluster of rocks and twigs. Digging through the browned leaves and boughs, he removed the family's coracle that he had hidden beneath them and lifted it into the water. As he packed the vessel with his bundle of clothes and satchel of food, he said, "Be careful, little one."

"And you," she said. "The Kield can be very frightening."

He laughed and hugged her, resting his chin on the top of her head. "No more frightening to me than what we might have to do, if the Drake Villae refuses my request."

"She won't refuse. She can't."

Again Edan laughed, this time sadly. He said nothing. Together brother and sister pushed the coracle into the water. The bottom of it scraped across silt and pebbles. He waded out knee-high and climbed in. The boat rocked. "I'm sorry to have to leave you and Edarra alone with Paudan, but I think it is best."

"We all agreed. You ought to try, Edan. We'll take care of Paudan."

"And yourselves, please," he said. Then he paddled off.

She watched him glide toward the opposite shore under the afternoon's cruel sun until he reached the middle of the lake. Then she glanced over to where the Lake Mother's island rose solitary from the green-gray waters. The island was covered with strange trees that grew nowhere else in Woodmill and that never shed their leaves. They hid the Mother's villa behind their dense, blue boughs.

Snow-Eyes squinted at the sky. It was clear and empty of clouds. No rain would be coaxed from it that day; the unspotted blue held no hope and no promise. The sun beat down. For a moment she glared at the island and thought, Wishing doesn't do any good. The Lake Mother isn't listening anymore. Maybe she isn't even there anymore!

As Snow-Eyes walked home, across the yellow grass field, she wondered whether the Lake Mother was even alive anymore— she might have returned to the Sea, to live with her sister, Death. Although Paudan had told her tales and tales wherein the Mother's blessing saved someone from sickness or sorrow, in all of Snow-Eyes's life, no wish she had ever made had come true. When Paudan had grown ill, Edan and Edarra had wished and wished on their stone— wished that their father would not suffer, that the rains would soon fall, that their crops might not die. Of course, Snow-Eyes would never touch the wishing stone herself, but she had knelt in the garden with her brother and sister and had added her plea to theirs.

Maybe, she thought as she walked across the field, maybe the stone is nothing more than a black rock, fancy-carved and useless. Maybe all of Paudan's stories are lies, as untrue as my not-dreams.

The sun set as she climbed over the fence onto a path. She brushed slivers of dry grass from her pants and listened to the locusts cricking in the bamboo. Grasshoppers skittered across the rutted, dusty path that rambled up to her home. The warm wind carried a hint of autumn—the odor of burnt leaves and mown hay.

As she came near to the villa, she saw a stranger standing before the iron-hinged front door. The door opened. The stranger went in.

Snow-Eyes stopped in the path and stared at the flat-roofed house's wide, square door as if it had changed in her absence to a thing foreboding and alien. She stared and thought, Who would be visiting us? Who is it? Even at a distance, the stranger was not a stranger to her. Snow-Eyes felt that she had seen the visitor before; someone familiar, but nameless in her memory. Who? She began to walk, then to run.

The front door was locked. She pounded on it once but, unwilling to wait for Edarra to come and open it, Snow-Eyes ran around to the kitchen. The back door was open. The kitchen was deserted. A fly buzzed in the window and all else was still. She hurried into the hall. As she walked past Paudan's workroom, the toys on his table seemed to stare at her. The round-eyed bullocks wrinkled their foreheads at her, the ebony owls scowled fierce and intensely. She nearly stopped. But shaking her head, she doubled her pace. A mouse hopped in fright away from her boots and scrambled into the atrium.

The stranger stood at the doorway to Paudan's bedroom. Her long, dark hair fell to her white jacket's belt. As Snow-Eyes crept nearer, the woman turned and glanced up, making her silver-mirror earrings swing and flash. She smiled.

Snow-Eyes stared. She remembered that wide and serious smile. She remembered a dark winter night, and the wishing stone looming before her and a dream about a bullock and a nightmare ... she stared at the nightmare visitor, who was, as she could see, not a dream after all. She whispered, "No."

The woman said nothing. She walked into the bedroom. Snow-Eyes waited for a few moments, her heart beating fast. The sudden remembrance held her because the evening and the wishing she had done on that winter midnight still felt to her unreal. Slowly she entered her father's room.

Edarra sat at Paudan's side, wiping his forehead with a dampened cloth. She rinsed the cloth in a dented basin and looked up at her sister, asking, "Edan has left?"

"He has." Snow-Eyes nodded. Pointedly, she walked around the woman who stood at the foot of the bed. "Did you let her in?" she asked Edarra.

"Who?" The older sister draped the cloth

she held over her father's forehead and frowned. "What are you talking about?"

"This woman—here."

Edarra's eyes widened. She stood and came over to her sister to lay her hand on Snow-Eyes's brow. "Have you been feeling ill, little one?"

"No."

"You feel warm to me. Warm. Why don't you lie down?"

The visitor said, "Amarra, your sister cannot see me. Only you can." She glanced at the bed. "Only you and Paudan will see me here." She moved to the opposite side of the room and sang in a quiet way,

My eyes cannot see you,
my darkling child.
You have fled from my side,
Oh, where can you be?
I am here, O my mother,
come touch me now, come run with me.
My face is cool, in the evening's shade.
My face is warm, in the morning's sun . . .

The song drifted in the close room like audible smoke, as heavy and sweet to Snow-Eyes as the breath of honeysuckle in summer.

Edarra said, "Here, little one, please, sit down."

"I am not ill," said Snow-Eyes impatiently.

Paudan opened his eyes and murmured, "Beya?"

"Yes."

Catching sight of the stranger, he smiled. But his smile was twisted and wry, full of some understanding that Snow-Eyes did not share. He said, "You've come."

"I said I would."

"Yes . . . for me. But it's too late, isn't it?"

Snow-Eyes cried out, "Too late? Paudan?"

At the sound of his daughter's voice, he turned his head. The effort made him cough until tears came. Edarra hurried to his side, wiped his face and said, gently, "Snow-Eyes has been here all along. Rest now. It isn't too late."

He said, "Watch your wishes, my children. Some of them are bound to be foolish and will only bring you pain."

The woman with the mirrored earrings said, "Do you think, Paudan, that we have been foolish to love? That you were wrong to wish for my love? We had as many seasons together and time—"

"Too short," he murmured, closing his eyes. "Wasted time."

"What is too short?" asked Edarra. She crouched close to the bed, her hands on her thighs.

"No time is ever wasted," said the stranger. "You would not learn to pay a season its

76

proper due. We had all the time to live together that I could give."

"Selfish," he said. He rocked his head back and forth so hard that the thin blanket on the bed slipped halfway to the floor. Snow-Eyes gathered it up and smoothed it across his chest. He clutched her hand and made her kneel close to the bed. She smelled the dry, stale odor of his age and his illness on his breath. She turned her head aside a little, ashamed that she did so, yet sickened by the odor. But she squeezed his crooked hand softly to reassure him.

He whispered, "You are my little one, Snow-Eyes. My daughter. Not hers. Don't forget me, don't forget that she left you—and me."

The stranger bent forward and grasped the wooden headboard. "I did my best . . . but I told you—"

He raised his head slightly off the pillow. "I don't believe you anymore, Beya Rete. I think that you had a choice, once, to come and visit us more often. Even to stay with me. If you had chosen to. But you never cared enough or loved me enough—"

"No! No!" She stroked his forehead. "Ah, Paudan . . ."

"Your mother," said Edarra. She touched her sister's arm. "Your mother . . . he thinks that she is here." She blinked and blinked and rubbed her eyes with one hand. She leaned to him and kissed his cheek. "I'm sorry, Paudan, I'm sorry but she's gone. She went away."

A tiny, grieving smile lifted his mouth. "Why?" He laid his head back down. "Why did you go?"

Snow-Eyes got up off her knees, holding tight to her father's hand. He stared at her. His face went pale under the brown spots of age. His dry skin was stretched tight and flat over his bones. He did not seem to see her and then he coughed, closed his eyes and made a deep, emptying sigh. His hand relaxed its grip.

Edarra clutched at the bedsheets and called to him, her expression going from blank to fearful.

Beya Rete stepped back from him.

Snow-Eyes could not look up to the woman's silver-white gaze because she knew now, with an awful, final certainty, that it would be her true mother's gaze—her own mother's gaze—that she would meet. She was afraid. She did not move.

Sudenly Beya Rete's dark hand searched out Paudan's again. For a moment they held onto one another, meshing their fingers tight until both the man's hand and the woman's whitened at the knuckles. Beya's earrings jangled like tiny, angry bells. Paudan placed his other hand on top of the stranger's and whispered, "I loved you, Beya. Why do you think I have stayed near the lake all these years, waiting, hoping—for you?"

Edarra frowned and said to her father, "What? What is it you want?"

Snow-Eyes forced herself to look up now. The blood pulsed in her temples and neck as she raised her head. She felt as if she might start to gasp for breath the way her father was gasping. But the woman no longer saw the girl at all. She was looking down at Paudan. Then she cried out and touched his closed eyes. She bowed her head.

Paudan grew utterly still.

Snow-Eyes watched for him to speak again but he did not move. She waited. She saw nothing beyond his stilled face, and she waited.

Edarra touched Paudan's cheek with the back of her hand. She pressed her forehead to the bed and began to cry softly.

Snow-Eyes knelt and put her arms around her sister's shoulders.

Sobbing, Edarra shook her head.

Finally, the younger sister stood again. She folded her father's stiff, bent hands and brushed back his thin hair. Then she looked around the room for her mother.

Beya Rete was gone.

Snow-Eyes stepped back from the death-bed. She went over to the window and pushed open the shutters. A breeze cleansed away the odor of sickness that clung to her and carried off the slight, sweet taste of honeysuckle in the room. It was twilight. The stars shone clearly. She stared at the path that led to the house, massaging her wrist where Paudan had held her so firmly.

There were two people at the very end of the path.

Snow-Eyes watched the two walk along for a few moments before she turned and ran out of the room, down the hall, past the carpenter's empty workroom and out the back door to the front stoop, where she stopped.

At the edge of the grass field, beyond the fence through which Snow-Eyes had climbed earlier, she saw the stranger, Beya Rete. The woman had her back to the girl and her white jacket was made as brilliant as snow by the blue moon's light. But she was not alone; someone walked beside her.

It was Paudan.

The couple walked slowly, or so it seemed, and yet they had gotten far from the house for so slow a pace. Paudan held Beya Rete's arm. Snow-Eyes ran a few steps down the path. Though she could see her father, he appeared to her insubstantial; as thin as fine-woven gauze, pale and naked. She hesitated and thought, How can Paudan be here? She glanced at the villa behind her and at its locked front door, and she remembered that the Lake Mother was the one who guided souls to the Sea.

Snow-Eyes jogged toward the grassy field, wanting to catch up with the couple—and yet, not wanting to, because she felt that meeting a soul would be a terrible thing indeed. Her father's soul. What would she do if she caught up with the couple? What could she say?

As Snow-Eyes gained the end of the road, the woman and the man reached the grove's edge. Then, quite suddenly, they melted into twilight's shadows among the bamboo trees. Snow-Eyes ran up to the fence. Her black shirt stuck to her sweaty chest. She tugged at it, then pulled it off and tied it around her waist. She scanned the darkening bamboo curtain for the couple, looking for a quick flutter of white. But she saw nothing. She climbed through the fence and ran across the field as fast as she could, pushing aside the high, dry grass. Disturbed grasshoppers left their meals and shot out from underfoot. Midges danced in the cool air, stung her shoulders and flew at her eyes. She pushed onward, despite the insects, until she could see Lake Wyessa beyond the grove, silver-smooth. She hurried toward the water, thinking that the woman must have reached her boat—but perhaps the couple might still be found before they left the shore.

Snow-Eyes ran again, dodging fallen trees and keeping her gaze on the lake. Leaves obscured the path, and low-hanging branches, made invisible by the dusk-light, scratched at her clothes and caught in her hair. The ground sloped downward.

In her urgency she tripped and fell head-long, rolling through the grass to the very edge of the water. She sat. Dizzy, out of breath, she leaned forward and closed her eyes. Her lip was cut. Both elbows stung. She had lost her shirt. Her back and chest prickled with little flecks of pain. She knew that she must have fallen over the brambles. She fisted one hand, opened her eyes and then rocked herself to her feet.

She had expected to see a coracle making fast across the rippling surface of the lake towad Trost. But the horizon was empty.

"Where are you?" she said aloud. Where could the man and the woman have gone?

A family of lake gillians burst out from the reeds and flew overhead, their wings as loud as sheets flapping on a clothes line. Mosquitoes worried the girl, and she slapped at their bites. Breathing hard from the shock of her fall, she stood gazing at the lake, unable to think of what to do. Her heart hammered in her throat. She sat down again.

The stars touched the dark sky with their cool fire, and an owl called, heralding night. She hugged her knees and winced at the pain of her cuts and bruises. The wind blew her hair across her face and she shivered—

where was her shirt? She felt at her waist for it, then remembered that she had lost it when she fell.

Reluctantly, urged on by the chilly air, she stood and hunted for the shirt. As she beat at the high grass for it, feeling miserable and sore, she thought of Paudan.

He was gone. If she went back home now and into his bedroom, she would find him lying in his bed, his hands folded as she had folded them, his hair parted as she had parted it, and he would be cold. She knew of Death. Though she had never seen Death's terrible face herself, she knew the hand of Death. Had she not found the old ram cold and stiff last winter? And the young birds that fell from their nests too soon, had she not found their broken bodies under the trees' shade? And the lambs lost questing for water during the drought, did she not grieve as the ewes grieved? She knew Paudan was dead and that somewhere on the other side of the world, past the sands of the Tenebrian Desert and beyond the heights of many mountains, his soul journeyed guided by . . . *her*, Beya Rete, who must be the Lake Mother. Snow-Eyes nodded. She had seen him, her father's soul, on his way to the Shore of Sansel's Sea. He would not be in the kitchen, peeking at supper; he would not be chopping nuts for the morn; he would not be whistling erratically to himself as he whittled in his workroom, nor would he be napping in the atrium. He would no longer ask for his pipe to be filled—indeed, it was sitting at that moment beside his bed, empty, the odor of bitter shag still clinging to the well-worn wooden bowl.

Snow-Eyes put on her shirt and sat in a small, grassy hollow. The mosquitoes bothered her less there, since a steady breeze from the lake's surface carried them off. She thought, Edarra did not see the woman . . . maybe Beya Rete was not there? Maybe she was a not-dream?

But Paudan saw her, came the answer from inside herself.

He had a fever. People see things, in a fever.

Then you have had a fever all your life—the way you not-dream all those things. Besides, Paudan thought that you saw her, too. And remember what she said? That Edarra could not see her. Only you and Paudan could. I wonder why. Is she the Lake Mother? Is she . . . is she really my mother?

"Who?" said Snow-Eyes aloud as she curled up on her side in the hollow. Her neck ached. She thought about going home. She ought not leave Edarra alone.

But she was so tired. The walk back seemed so long, back through the dark grove, stumbling, back across the grass, in the dark, all alone. Who knows what she might step on? And how was she to find her way, in the dark? She rolled over and stared up at the moon.

Why didn't Paudan ever tell me that my mother was also the Lake Mother? Why doesn't she look like the portrait in the front room? Snow-Eyes turned over on her side again. A ground fog crept in all the water and curled into the grassy hollow with her. The moon's light was soft but bright, and she closed her eyes to it, covering her face with her arm. The bamboo leaves whispered and spun on their twigs. The lake water lapped. The owl cried again. Despite all the questions to which she had no answers, Snow-Eyes slept.

4

A Rope
of Indigo Rings

A CHIME RANG. A chime rang, a small but insistent chime rang over and over. Wakened by this sound, Snow-Eyes stretched and blinked several times. The day was dim and cloudly, the fog still heavy on the land.

The chime stopped. She stared down at her dirty, bloodied hands, crooked in the grass beside her. A trailing end of her long hair lay tangled near a contingent of fat black ants that crawled chaotically in the dew. She sat. Her neck was stiff and her forearms were bruised. She yawned widely, then looked at her scabbing elbows and winced; the skin around the new scabs was pinkish, swollen and tender.

She was surprised at how cloudy and dark the sky was. She yawned again, stretching. The matted grass crushed under her smelled sweet.

Lake gillians appeared suddenly from the far side of Wyessa. They circled once, and one by one, they landed in the water, arching their black wings and sliding across the surface. She rubbed one eye, took off her shirt and shook it out.

The small chime rang again, startling her. This time she knew that the sound was more than a part of her dream—or a not-dream, as she had thought it to be. She turned. At the lip of the hollow, Edarra and the woman, Beya Rete, stood together. The chiming came from a rope of indigo liganuli rings that Edarra held. She was counting the rings. The petrified wood clinked softly, like polished chalcedony, as each ring slid from Edarra's hand to the knotted end of the rope.

Snow-Eyes stood and yanked her shirt quickly over her head. She called, "Edarra?"

Her sister stopped counting the liganuli to stare at Snow-Eyes and whisper, "You're awake . . ." The older girl turned to Beya Rete. "You said she wouldn't wake!"

Beya replied, "I expected that she would not. It is too soon. But . . ."

"Soon?" Snow-Eyes squinted in the dim light, glancing from face to face. Then she demanded of her sister, "Who is this woman? Is she the Lake Mother? Do you know if she is my mother? Who is she?"

Edarra stared at the rope of indigo rings that she held and said, "This is the Lake Mother's daughter, to whom you now belong."

Snow-Eyes caught her breath, speechless. Edarra's answer was unexpected and wrong, wrong ... Edarra should have said just, "The Lake Mother." Not ... not *that*, not what she had just said.

Seemingly unmindful that she had made the wrong answer, Edarra tied the rope of indigo to her belt and ran her fingers down the buttons of her shirt nervously. She said, "I found her out here with you this morning. When you didn't come back last night, I was afraid and came looking. Instead of you, I found her ... she said she would trade me enough to buy the villa from the Drake, if I would give you to her. So I decided—"

"You decided? What about me? Give back the rope and let's go home."

"No," said Edarra Her voice cracked. "The villa ..."

"Edarra!"

"No."

Snow-Eyes took a step back and then turned to run. But the woman jumped down into the hollow and caught the girl around the waist, dragging her to the ground. Snow-Eyes cried out, sprang back to her feet and fought to get past the woman and run away. But Beya Rete held on. Snow-Eyes scratched at her and tried to pry open the strong fingers. She tried shaking the woman off and pulled her wrists upward. "Let me go!"

Beya Rete held on. "Stop it, child!"

Snow-Eyes stood still; not because the woman had said to, but because something strange was happening ... it was getting darker and darker, as if night were coming in rather than the dawn. She frowned and turned to her sister. "Edarra, did you say that it was morning?"

"Of course it's morning. Can't you see?"

"No-o." Snow-Eyes flinched. Beya Rete let go of her wrists. Confused, she did not move. She blinked, but it seemed to make no difference whether her eyes were open or closed. She touched her eyelids and blinked again. She shook her head from side to side. But there was no glimmer at all, not even a whisper of light in the dark. She sat down, pulled her knees up to her chin and wrapped her arms around her legs. She felt herself shaking.

"Snow-Eyes?" It was Edarra's voice. "What's wrong with you?"

The woman in white said gently, "You have gotten your wish, Edarra ... go on home now."

"But—you said that you wouldn't hurt her! You said you would take her to your villa and treat her as you would treat a daughter. Snow-Eyes? What has happened?"

"I—I can't see ..."

"Go to your home, Edarra," said Beya. "You have wished and wished to buy it, isn't this so? And the last time you made the wish, you said, 'No matter what, whatever it costs, however I can,' didn't you?"

"Yes, but—"

"A wish is always filled by the Lake Mother. It may take time, you may need wait for her answer or look for it in a place you did not expect. She may answer your wish in a manner you do not understand. But she always answers. I am the Lake Mother's daughter. I do as I am bidden, and I was bidden to fulfill your wish."

"No!" cried Snow-Eyes. Sick with anger and fright, she jumped up toward her sister, her arms outstretched. "Don't leave me!" she cried.

"Oh—" said Edarra. She grabbed the younger girl and hugged her close. With her free hand, she yanked the liganuli from her belt, making the rings chime. "I don't want these!" she said. "I was wrong! Give me back my sister."

There was silence. Snow-Eyes hid her face against Edarra's shoulder, pressing her cheek against the rough wool. She was trembling, and she could feel her sister breathing hard. Then she felt herself being pulled away. She grabbed at the prickly weave of Edarra's jacket, and she felt her sister's hands clutching at her waist, but the pull was inexorable. Snow-Eyes was not strong enough to resist—suddenly, she was snatching and grabbing at nothing.

"Where are you?" whispered Edarra. Her voice sounded half-strangled.

"Here! Here!" cried Snow-Eyes frantically. "Edarra!"

"No, child," said Beya Rete in a flat and final tone. "She does not see us. She cannot hear you anymore."

"Snow-Eyes?" said Edarra and then she cried out, a moan of grief.

"Edarra!" Snow-Eyes groped, arms flailing, until she heard a scuffle in the grass and the rustling of footsteps, running away. "Edarra! Wait!" She tried to chase after the footsteps, but strong hands held her back.

"Stop. Your sister has gone."

"No! Oh, no, please . . ." Snow-Eyes cried to the wind. "Oh, please, come back . . ." But there was no answer. Feebly she tried to push the stranger away, she tried to escape the scent of honeysuckle and the soft, deep voice. "Please, please, let me go."

"Ah, but what about your wish? I have come to answer your wish, as well as your sister's."

"I have never made a wish!"

"You have, child. Think on it."

"I have not—" Snow-Eyes stopped to consider. She remembered only that she had knelt with her brother and sister in the atrium when they had asked for an end to

the drought ... but ... she remembered
something else ... night, wind, snow. Silver eyes and silver earrings. Had she not
asked for three things? And had not Paudan
hugged her close afterward ... and the
black stone and three wishes instead of one.
As she remembered all that had passed long
ago on that night that the woman in white
had first visited, Beya Rete spoke, saying,
"You asked that you might not be so little,
that your brother and sister would not scold
you, and that you might grow up to be—"

"You. It was you. It was not a dream ..."

"No, I am not a dream. Come." The
woman touched the girl's shoulder again.
"Come, take my hand. I will be your eyes,
now."

But Snow-Eyes did not move. "Please,"
she whispered. "I don't want to go with
you. Give me back my sight and let me—"

"Child." The woman's tone was sharp with
impatience. "I can't do that."

"Why? You took it away, didn't you?"

"Yes. But I cannot give it back. Listen,
now, we don't have much time. We are late;
I have been away from home too long."

"Home? Where's—"

"Listen to me. Many seasons ago, the Lake
Mother—"

"Aren't you the—"

"Hush now and listen!"

Snow-Eyes swallowed hard.

Beya Rete sighed. "Seasons and seasons ago," she said, "the Lake Mother, whose name is Trost, chose four women from among the people of all Gueame to be her guardians and servitors. No one knows, not even we who serve Trost today, just how those first four daughters were chosen. But they became the companions of the Lake Mother. And after she was bereft of that child who had been begot by wild Aenan, the chosen four became a solace to her. Eventually she decided to give these daughters a portion of her own power. It is told to us that the Lake Mother asked—" Beya halted her story. She hesitated for some moments before she said, "It is told to us that the Lake Mother asked nothing; she came one evening to her daughters and touched their eyes with her tears. While they slept, Trost gave them each the tears of her own heart, wrung from the sadness of an ancient life. When the women woke, they were blind."

"You—is that what you have done to me?"

"Yes. Last night, I touched your eyes with the tears of Trost."

"But why? Why did she—why did you—"

"Because, child, you were born with a strong gift—as I was, as my mother was, as were all the children of our blood; Trost's blood. Even when you were very young, I could feel the gift in you, waiting for the day when Trost's tears would make it grow. We call the gift *insight* because those who have it may reach into the dream-time to make the strange and unreal real. To make wishes come true."

"Is that ... is that like not-dreaming?" whispered Snow-Eyes.

Beya Rete laughed. "Yes, I imagine that insight is not-dreaming. But you must not think that this gift is rare. No, many people, especially those born in Woodmill, have a slight touch of it; even your sister does, though she might deny it. I've met many who've denied it. The gift frightens. It frightened Paudan's Eda. He learned to deny himself the use of his gift, for her. Thus he slowly lost it, as you might lose the use of your legs, if you never walked upon them."

"But I'm blind!" said Snow-Eyes.

"The blindness is not forever. It is merely a time of waiting and of patience. Trost's tears will make your insight grow stronger and wider. But as the tears work in you, you will not be able to see; this is because Trost wishes you to understand the pain that she endured when her first child was stolen from her by her jealous brother, Death."

"Brother?"

But Beya did not appear to hear the girl's remark. She said, "Someday, Amarra, you shall be twice-strong with insight. You will

learn to use your gift. By custom, I am
bidden to give my daughter the tears so
that her eyes will be made over into dream-
eyes and so that she will be made over into
a servitor of Trost."

Snow-Eyes folded her hands tightly. She
frowned and then asked, "Does that mean I
shall see again someday?"

"Yes, yes," said the woman impatiently.
"When you make your first vow of obedience to Trost—upon her own wishing stone—
on that day you shall be reborn as a servitor, and on that day you shall see again."
Beya took hold of the girl's hands and un-
folded them. "Come," she said.
"What if . . . what if I don't want—"

"Amarra, you are my daughter. Paudan
has kept you from me too long. Now it is
time that you came home."

"My home is here."

There was a pause. Beya said softly, "Not
anymore, child." She began to walk toward
the lake, urging the girl along beside her.

Snow-Eyes thought to resist and to dig
her heels into the earth; to fight. But she
did not. What can I do but go with this
woman, who is my mother? she thought. I
can't run, if I can't see. And where would I
run to? Edarra could not help me against
the Lake Mother's strength, and Edan is far
away . . . and what could he do that Edarra
could not have done?

So, walking with a hesitant shuffle, Snow-Eyes followed her mother and wondered how much time would need pass before she was given back her sight . . . and what would it be like to have her eyes made over into dream-eyes? If it meant seeing odd creatures moving in the dark, like the ones that had peered at her on the beach of her blooding, she wasn't sure that she wanted them. And what did it mean to be a servitor? She thought that it might not be pleasant, this making-over; in fact, she was sure that it was not going to be pleasant. And why had she never heard of these servitors of Trost? Paudan had never spoken of them, nor had any of the books on the shelves. Books! Snow-Eyes made a small whimper of despair as she realized that a blind girl could not read.

"Hush," said the woman.

Snow-Eyes was about to ask if she might not refuse the tears of Trost somehow and give them back, when water splashed her pants, seeping through the gut-lashed seams of her boots. As she jumped backward, she remembered that she had not seen a boat earlier; nothing at all, neither coracle nor river-punt.

She said, "What—" but as she spoke, everything changed.

She was falling forward—or backward? . . . She kicked to find a footing, grabbed at air and tried to break her tumble with her shoulder but ... she had no arms. They were shrunken, mere fingerless stumps. Her legs were gone, too. Yet, she had something there in their place, something thick and long and powerful ... a finned tail. Where her arms had been, pectoral fins grew. The air tasted metallic, like the water from the Kield pump, tainted with iron ... except, she was not breathing air. Her chest did not expand and contract with the exercise of lungs; instead, gills opened and closed. She had no voice. Floating, suspended above the earth, voiceless, legless, she listened for Beya Rete, but heard instead many, many sounds, none of them human—she was sure of that. A warm, rippling current washed over her, like a fan of heat waves rising off a road in summer. Overhead, huge, noisy gillians dove among the black-rooted pondweed. Terrified now and still blind, Snow-Eyes floated passively until she felt something nudge her as the yearling lambs often did when she fell asleep in their pasture. She nearly darted away from the nudge. What if it were some lake creature, come to eat the blind and torpid silvern that she had become?

A voice that was not her own but was nevertheless inside her head said, "Wait for me and then follow." Snow-Eyes waited; after a moment, she was nudged again.

A smooth, scaled body flowed against her.

The long body then began to swim. Snow-Eyes felt wavelets, made by the other's movement, tickle her. She followed the vibrations, touching the other now and then for the reassurance that she was not alone.

As the two moved along, the girl-who-was-a-fish began to feel her way through the water and found that she could swim easily past objects that she could not see. She could do this because she could *hear* the objects—a rock, a school of minnows, a half-sunken tree—she could hear their shapes and sizes by uncanny sound pictures. The pictures were confusing, but not at all strange. And so, in consequence, she did not try to puzzle out where the pictures came from, but glided beneath the green-gray waters beside the woman-fish, across the length of Lake Wyessa, toward Trost.

5

The Women of Lake Wyessa

GASPING FOR AIR, Snow-Eyes found herself standing in the sand. She was no longer a fish. Water weighted her clothes and streamed off her. She kneaded her arms and wiggled her toes in the sand.

"Here," said Beya Rete. She took hold of the girl's hand and let her up from the lake's edge. Snow-Eyes could feel the sun on her face and shoulders. The land inclined upward, and she stumbled over a rock and some twigs. Gaining her balance again, she stood still, afraid she might step into a hole or stub her toes.

"Here," said Beya. "Sit down."

Snow-Eyes did as she was asked and let herself be stripped of all her wet clothes. The sun soon warmed her clammy skin. As she stretched out in the sand, she flexed her feet and arched her back, glad to have her arms and legs again, glad to be herself again.

After a few minutes she asked, "Why did you do that? What is wrong with a boat?"

The woman laughed. "Nothing's wrong with a boat. I simply don't like them. I prefer swimming."

"But! But our clothes are all wet!"

"They will dry soon enough. If the sun had not been shining, I might have made us both bats instead."

"Well," said the girl in a low, glum voice, "you might have warned me." She turned over onto her stomach and winced. The little bramble cuts in her neck and torso stung. She propped herself up on her elbows.

"How should I have warned you, Amarra? Would you have truly believed me if I had said, 'Now, child, I am going to make you into a silvern so that we may swim to Trost'?"

"No . . ." Snow-Eyes scooped up a handful of dry sand and let it sift through her fingers. "Why didn't Edarra know you as my mother? She should have—"

"Because I willed it so," said Beya flatly. Her voice sounded hard, as hard as the rock that the wishing stone was carved of. "She thinks that you have been taken away by the Lake Mother—as you have. It is an honor, Amarra. You might not think so now, but you will." She lowered her voice. "You will."

A few moments of silence passed between

the two. At last Snow-Eyes asked, "Why do you call me Amarra?"

"Because it is your name."

"My birth-name."

"Yes."

"Paudan always called me Snow-Eyes." The girl spread her hands out flat and rested her forehead on the warmed earth. "Did you choose the name Amarra for me?"

"We both did, Paudan and I. He said that it meant, 'from the blue shore.'"

Snow-Eyes nodded and drew her knees up under her stomach. She brushed a coating of sand off her breasts, rubbed her hands together and said, "You left us. You left him—and me."

"I had to leave. Paudan knew why. I told him how it would be. But he did not wish to listen." She sighed, and her earrings tinkled faintly. "Did he not tell you?"

"No, nothing."

The woman said sharply, "Nothing at all? What do you mean?"

"He told me about the Lake Mother, of course . . ." Snow-Eyes drew back from the metallic jingle of the mirror earrings. "But what you said earlier about servitors, and blindness, he never mentioned that."

"No, he would not have spoken about the tears of Trost. He did not know of them."

"Also," said Snow-Eyes, "he refused to tell me about my mother. He never even told me her—your—name. Why? Why did you leave? Where have you been?"

The woman whispered, "He was angry . . ."

Snow-Eyes opened her mouth to answer, then closed it and stopped to think about her father. She remembered the way he had told the stories about the Lake Mother—with passion and love. She remembered the way he spoke of his past; his gaze would move around the room uneasily, resting on a wall or out the window. She knew that he was looking at places that Snow-Eyes had never visited. And yet she felt as if she had gone to those places because the words he used to describe them—the pictures he painted with those words, the love that he felt—made the past come to life for her—as if it had been her own past, not his. She remembered how his mouth would form a smile and how he would speak in the accents of a remembered voice and then would answer himself, as if answering a visionary guest. When he told a tale, he breathed being into it—his being, his life and his loneliness. She said, "I don't think he was so much angry, as alone."

"I have been alone, too," said Beya. "I wonder if he ever thought of that. Of how lonely I have been, for his touch."

"What does it matter now?" said Snow-Eyes bitterly. Her throat felt tight. "He's . . . he's . . ."

"It matters."

"You could have come home."

"No."

"Why? Why?"

The woman stood up. "When I made my first vow to Trost, I pledged her that I would do her bidding. Her work came before all else. I could not visit Paudan or you as often as I wished. I did not have that choice, not if I—" She paused. "I did not have the choice. Paudan fought me over this. He kept me from you."

"How? He wouldn't. I don't believe it."

Beya did not answer. A moment later, Snow-Eyes felt the bundle of her dried clothing dropped into her lap. She fumbled with the sleeves of her tunic. Shaking it out by the shirttails, she pulled it over her head, then stood and put her pants on. She could hear that the woman was also dressing. She took a step toward the sound of the other's rustling clothes as she tied the drawstring of her trousers. She said, "You are my mother?"

"Yes, child."

"You are—you're so young. I mean, Paudan was not young."

"Time passes differently for me—for we who are servitors." Beya handed Snow-Eyes her soft black boots. They were still damp. "I was born in Kield Woodmill; a marke-

teer's daughter. I told you my name once—
do you remember it?''

''I didn't, not until Paudan said . . . before he died, he spoke to you and called you
Beya.''

''Beya Rete. My mother is also a daughter
of Trost, as I am now. When I was a little
girl, she left my father—as all of us must
leave our families one day—and we returned
here, to Trost's villa I missed my father, but
I learned, oh! many things, the ancient powers of dream-seeing, the use of insight—
and stories. Many of them, which I will
teach you, if you are good.'' She sighed,
then laughed. ''Would you like to learn how
to make yourself into a silvern? Would you
like to know how to step into your 'not-
dreams' and make them true? Would you
like to answer wishes?''

''I—no, I don't know.'' Snow-Eyes sat
down to put on her boots. Beya Rete was
offering her a chance to be what she had
dreamt of being ever since she was a little
girl—to have power like the Lake Mother
and to become strong. Suddenly, though,
Snow-Eyes was not altogether sure that she
wanted that power. She doubted she was
clever enough to learn to change herself
into a silvern. And she had seen just how
Edarra's wish had been fulfilled.

Yet, she thought, perhaps . . . what if I
could make myself into a fish—or a night-

owl? Unaware that she was speaking aloud, Snow-Eyes murmured, "I might go home—"

"This is your home now, Amarra," said Beya. "You are one of Trost's chosen daughters, as I am. Paudan tried to keep you from me, by not telling you of your heritage. He was mistaken. You belong—"

Snow-Eyes waited for her mother to continue. When she did not, the girl said, "But, why didn't you come home, just once, and tell me about Trost? I can't believe that Paudan would have stopped—"

"Listen!"

A bell was ringing. Then another bell rang, soon a third, and Snow-Eyes knew them to be the bells of seasonchange. She listened closely, wondering if her name would be spoken inside the light carillon . . .

"Hurry," said Beya. "Get your boots on. I am late, and Lammar is angry."

"Who is Lammar?"

"Hurry, hurry—"

Snow-Eyes jammed her feet into the shoes and tied up the laces as swiftly as she could manage. Each eye-hole for the laces seemed to hide from her fingers, and the more she hurried, the more they hid. At last she got them all done up and stood. Beya took her hand again, and they began to walk at a quick clip. The earth changed underfoot from loose sand to hard-packed dirt and rock. Wind sighed in the tree boughs and carried a strange, clean scent—a sharp scent, like the mint that Edan grew for summer tea. The bell-song continued, growing louder and louder as they walked.

"What are we late for?" asked Snow-Eyes. "Who is Lammar?"

"You will meet her soon—and mind you don't bother her with any foolish questions. If you have to ask something, be sure to ask me. Always. Lammar seems patient, but she is not. At the moment, she is angry."

Snow-Eyes nodded, and bit the edge of her upper lip. Where was she being led? Why was Lammar so fearsome to Beya? What would happen to them?

The path began to incline upward, but Beya did not slacken the pace. Snow-Eyes nearly had to run to keep up with the woman's long stride. Panting, she asked, "Why . . . why don't you make us both into birds? Then we c-could fly wherever it is that we are going."

"No, no, I'm not strong enough to do a dream-change twice."

They climbed. The sun beat down on Snow-Eyes's shoulders and she thought, We must have quit the woods now. But still they did not slow.

The path's ascent leveled. The wind-sighing of the trees had been replaced by the deafening bells of seasonchange. Snow-Eyes clutched Beya's hand tightly. The top of her head felt scorched, and she was thirsty. Her stomach ached. But she feared to complain and so walked on.

Finally, Beya halted and shouted, "There is a staircase here!"

Snow-Eyes nodded and stepped up the stone stairs one at a time, following Beya's guidance. She could even feel the bells' toll through the soles of her boots. The ground vibrated with it. A moment later, shade lifted the weight of the sun's heat from her head and shoulders. A creaking sound and the sudden sweep of cool air on her face told her that a door had been opened. She held back a little when Beya stepped forward so that she might walk behind her mother. Inside, it was cool and dank. The bells sounded distant, and as the door closed, it shut out the sound of the carillon.

"Where are we?" asked Snow-Eyes. Her voice seemed tiny and hollow; so changed did it sound that she wondered for an instant if it was truly her own voice.

"No more questions now," said Beya peremptorily.

The two walked down a narrow passage. By stretching out one hand, Snow-Eyes could feel that the walls were made of smooth and slimy stone. The roof was low because she could touch that, too, and the air had become musty and chill. She had a terrible feeling that she would reach the end of the passage only to be met by a blank wall and the clink of metal on rock, and then hear a slow ha! ha!—just like a tale she had once read, an ancient tale from another time about a mossy passageway and a drear death.

But their footsteps' echoes grew louder and louder, and the hunched walls opened onto a wider space—a room? Snow-Eyes reached out her hand before her, but she felt nothing except that the air was warmer. She was about to ask Beya where they were now, when an odd hum and click behind her made her jump. She half-turned toward the sound.

Someone said, "Too long, Beya."

Snow-Eyes shivered and stepped close to her mother's side. Whoever had spoken had a low voice, as low as a man's, yet lilting and melodic. Echoes scuttled around the wide room like sound-mice. She wondered if the voice belonged to the Lake Mother or—

"I'm sorry, Lammar," answered Beya. "I had not meant to stay so long in Adeo. I had no idea that there was drought in Woodmill, nor that Paudan was ill. And of course I wished to speak to Amarra about her eyes before I brought her home."

"Amarra," murmured the stranger. Two firm hands grasped the girl's shoulders, and a cool, fleshy cheek was pressed to her face.

"We have waited for you, my child. I am Lammar."

"And I, Verlie," said another woman. Her voice sounded as if she was quite young. She, too, hugged Snow-Eyes.

Then a third woman spoke, "I am Parella." This last voice ranged somewhere between the first two. She kissed Snow-Eyes lightly on the forehead. Her lips were cold.

"We are the servitors of Trost," said Lammar.

Snow-Eyes turned her head from side to side, trying to locate the women by the sound of their voices. But the whispering echoes of the room confused her. Finally she managed to say, "My name is Snow-Eyes."

"Eyeseyeseyes," repeated the room, until the girl put her hands over her ears.

"Amarra," said Beya crossly. "Her given name is—"

"We would be pleased to share a meal with you tonight, Snow-Eyes," said the woman named Lammar. "But Beya is late in coming home, and we must work before we may eat. The drought has been terrible."

"I am sorry," said Beya. "I didn't think I would need to take Paudan to Trost . . . I did not know, Lammar! I tarried in Adeo, yes, but there was no news of the drought—"

"And you did not answer my dream-calls

to you. Yes, you are sorry. Always you are sorry. Come."

"How should I have known to answer? You are forever bothering me with nothings—"

"Nothings? Yes, yes, well . . . come along now. This is not a nothing."

Someone took Snow-Eyes by the hand. Swallowing her questions, the girl walked with the women across the whispering room and up a staircase, then down a corridor. her soft-shod feet brushed a slick floor and made her feel unsteady, as if she were slipping across ice. At the end of the corridor, she was taken into another room. This place smelled of sunstars and was much warmer than the corridor. She caught her foot on the edge of something, but one of the women steadied her and then handed her onto a bed that had no legs. She sat down.

"You are tired," said Lammar. "Sleep. Here is a blanket, beside you."

"Wait for us," said Beya. She gave Snow-Eyes a large, round fruit and a half-loaf of warm bread. The girl held the apple and loaf, though by now she was not in the least bit hungry. Her stomach had closed up, as had her throat. She wanted a drink of water. She wanted to know: "Are you . . . you're not going to leave me?"

"Only for a short time," said Beya. "Sleep.

You're tired. When you wake up, we shall be back, for supper."

"Oh, please, don't leave me alone! Please ..."

"Hush, now ..." whispered one of the women, and then the door clicked and they were gone.

Snow-Eyes called to each of them, speaking their names tentatively. But her voice was eaten by her silence, and her cries went unanswered. She sat there on the legless bed, balancing the large apple in one hand and the bread in the other. For a few moments, she was silent. Then, she said, "Oh, Paudan ..." She told herself she would not cry, she would not! But a sob at last forced its way through her pressed lips, her breath caught in her dry, ragged throat, and she could not stop the tears. Hiccuping, she put the bread and fruit down on the blanket near her and curled up on the bed, folding her hands under her cheek.

In a little while, she calmed herself by thinking of her father and of how Beya had said she had taken him to Trost. Trost would no doubt take him straight to the Sea of Sansel's Net. As a child, Snow-Eyes had learned from Paudan that if the dead one's soul carried falsities upon it that had caused another's pain, then that soul would not be able to leave the Shore easily. It would not join the Sea of Sansel's Net, where time was nothing but a memory. However, if the soul had truth and if mercy touched it often, then the soul would not need to wait lonely on the barren Shore, calling out to the ones it had hurt for forgiveness. Snow-Eyes knew her father had been good and kind; he would not need to wander on the Shore. But just as this thought came to her, she heard what sounded like a moan inside her head—a roil of human anguish that echoed like the sea's shadow-voice caught in the twisting corridors of a shell. She sat up.

The sound vanished. She forced herself to think instead of her home and her bed with its blue blanket. Was it evening there? The greedy chickens would miss her tonight. The sheep would bleat for her, but she would not answer. Her little, narrow bed would be cold and empty. And what of Edarra? Was she making her own supper and eating it, solitary, in the villa where Paudan's body lay quiet and abandoned? What of Edan? What would he say when he came home from Woodmill to find his little one sold away for a rope of indigo rings and the promise of buying the villa from the Drake?

Snow-Eyes dried her sunburnt cheeks on the coverlet. Maybe, she thought, Edan will come after me. She felt around on the bed for the apple. She tried to bite into it and found the rind far tougher than any apple skin should be. She finally scored it with a thumbnail and peeled back the fruit's hide. A shower of tiny, soft kernels, like corn, fell into her hand. She tasted one. It was juicy and tart. She pulled at the fruit rind, eating the seeds in big handfuls and smearing her face with their juice.

When she had finished both fruit and loaf, she felt better. The ache in her forehead had gone; she was warmer. She thought of Edarra again. She could almost see her sister sitting at the kitchen table, with the darkness of the summer's eve all around. She would have her candle's meager light and the locusts' song for company as she sat and ate her cold potato soup.

Snow-Eyes crawled to the end of the bed and stood up. Where, exactly, was she? She put her arms out before her so that she might feel her way and keep herself from knocking into walls or tables or what-not. Beya had told her to wait, but what harm could she do by exploring the room?

She took one step, then another and nudged a table with her thigh. She ran her hands along the smooth surface. Her fingertips brushed the edge of something rough. Carefully, she touched it again. Straw—no, tougher and splintery. A basket. Grasping one end, she picked it up and reached inside. Dry, soft flakes, like paper, only smoother, crinkled between her fingers. She sniffed— sunstar petals, dried. She put the basket down and started to walk across the room, searching for the door to the hall. She slid her hands along the curving wall. But she could not find a handle, or a door . . . where? She leaned—and suddenly, the wall was gone. She stepped forward and found herself in the corridor.

Now what? Should she do as she had been told and wait? Should she try to sleep? She was not tired. She decided to go on.

Silence attended her as she inched her way down the hall, keeping one hand on the concave wall. She tried to remember from which direction she had come with the servitors, because she thought she might return to the whispering, echoing room and find the front door. She did not know what she would do if she got outside again. Maybe I'll just sit in the sun and wait for someone to come. I'll tell them that I won't go back inside until I can talk to Trost and ask her for myself if I can't give back the tears. Thinking on this possibility, Snow-Eyes stopped to wonder whether Trost actually lived in the villa, since she had not met the Lake Mother when she had met the others.

The hall seemed much longer than Snow-Eyes remembered it. She worked her way past wall seams, searching for the staircase. There were no windows but she touched heavy, hanging drapery at intervals. Tapping one booted foot quietly before the other as she went, she found a staircase and wound her way down it, keeping her hand before her to guide her way. At the bottom of the stairs she hesitated. Should she turn left or right? Which way? She decided to take the right. It has to be this way, she thought. She stepped . . .

. . . and walked into a wall. Stunned, she yelped and then shut her mouth on the cry. Rubbing the bridge of her stinging nose, she coughed from the pain. Carefully she put her hands on the offending obstacle and thought, We couldn't have come *through* this wall . . . no. We must have come from the left, though I don't remember it. Now, let me see . . . we climbed the stairs, a long hall, then the room with the sunstar petals . . . should be simple!

Reluctantly, she turned to her left, knowing that she was lost already. She went on, down another flight of stairs and up two, around corners, through rooms, some large, some small. Nothing felt familiar. No door opened onto a dank and chilly passage. She could not even find the room where the women had bid her sleep.

Soon, although she had no way of truly knowing, Snow-Eyes was sure that the hour had gotten late and that the time had gone past supper. She sat at the top of some staircase—had she climbed up it or down it earlier? She did not know. She was lost.

The Lake Mother's villa was so big and twisted! Not a simple square, like her own home. She leaned against a hanging rug's edge and wondered, Will Beya or anybody be able to find me? Am I lost forever?

"Maybe I'll starve ..." she said in the same voice that she had not recognized as he own in the dank, stone corridor—a voice made small and timorous by fear. "Oh, hush," she told herself. "Someone will find you."

Will they? she cried inwardly and then stood. "Beya?" she said aloud. "Beya?" If she called long enough, perhaps the echoes would carry her voice to her mother's ears. "Beya!"

But silence swallowed her cry. The name she called seemed to jump from her mouth into the air, but the sound of it died immediately, like a flame lit but then instantly killed by a playful, nasty wind. There were no echo-mice here, no whispering repetitions to take her plea down the stairs. She called and called, too tired and hungry to wander the halls alone, but too frightened to sit in the eerie silence and do nothing.

Footsteps?

"Beya?" The girl's voice croaked and shook. Was it a footstep that she had heard, or ... what if her cry had called up some odd creature out of some hidden attic room? The villa was so large that many, many people—or things—might be living in it, hidden in its depths like the sea dragon hid in the sea. What if it were Trost herself a-coming ... what if it were Trost's sister, Death?

The footsteps came closer. Someone—or something—was climbing the stairs below, tap, tap, tapping closer and closer.

She whispered, "Beya?" but her voice was nearly inaudible.

Tap ... tap ...

Snow-Eyes edged backward. Her heart leapt and beat hard in her throat like a swallowed bird might. She backed away, and a small, strangled noise came from her ...

And Beya said, "I'm here, child. It's all right. I'm here."

With a shuddering sigh, Snow-Eyes hugged her mother's waist and let herself be rocked to and fro. She smelled the sweet honeysuckle oil on Beya's skin and the damp warmth of the woman's wet hair, and she murmured, "I was lost."

Beya nodded as she continued to rock her daughter. "You ought to have waited."

Snow-Eyes let her eyes close. She was exhausted; all her limbs felt light and weak.

A soft pattering overhead, like the pecking of a thousand birds roused her. She cocked her head. "What is that sound?"

Her mother laughed. "Why, it is raining. Lammar told you we had work to do. I am truly sorry about the drought, but I had no idea ... and as you see, there must be four of us here, to call in the rains. It is hard to make the rain fall. Three cannot do it."

A roll of thunder rumbled overhead, and the patterning became faster and heavier. Beya slid her arm down to the girl's waist and led her to the end of the hall.

"Here," she said.

A gust of cool air blew on Snow-Eyes's face. Raindrops spattered against the sill. She put her hand out the tiny window. Chill and heavy drops hit her palm. She put out her other hand, making a cup with her palms to catch the rain in a pool and drank the water in one draught to soothe her sore, dry throat.

6

The Heart of the House

HOME. The longer Snow-Eyes lived with the servitors of Trost, the more she thought about her flat-roofed home. Time and time again she wondered how her greedy band of chickens fared without her, or if the lambs she had helped to birth were full grown.

Most of all, she wondered about Edan and Edarra—didn't they miss her as much as she missed them? Didn't they care? Sadly, over time, she decided that her brother and sister must have forgotten her, since neither of them had come looking for her, since neither of them had come knocking on the villa door.

Even so, sometimes as she went about her chores, cleaning the kitchen floor or washing clothes, she would imagine the day of her homecoming. She would see herself walking up the road to the flat-roofed villa, and see the great many tears shed and Edarra asking forgiveness. Sometimes she imagined that she had gotten her sight back. More often she simply dreamt that she had never grown up at all—that she was a little child again, barefoot and running furiously across the grass to Edan, launching herself into his arms.

Yet all these envisioned reunions were shaded with sadness, because Paudan would appear in them and then she would remember that he had died. His absence made the memory of her home strange and unreal to her.

And, too, he would come into her dreams at night—when she could remember her dreams, which was seldom now, unlike the vivid nights she had spent as a little child. Paudan never said anything, never scolded or reminded or admonished as he had in life. Mostly he would sit in a corner of the dream and whittle. When she woke in the morning, she felt as if he might still be there in the room with her, sitting on the edge of her bed as he had often done when she was a child. She remembered how safe she had felt with him there, safe and no longer afraid of the dark.

Still, Snow-Eyes had little time for sadness and imaginings. She had many a task to do. She helped to bake bread or to make candles—work she had once done at home swiftly and with grace, but could barely do it all now because of her blindness. All of her days were filled with a thousand trials. She had to learn how to do everything in a new way. Everything! From dressing at dawn to washing up at night. There were so many tasks, too! The women of Trost were the caretakers of a thousand tiny rituals. Each day and nearly every moment was sacred to Trost in a different manner. The work had to be done just so—for instance, the daily chore of setting out a loaf of bread and a jug of water in the weaving room's window: the window was never closed; the bread had to be fresh each day; the water jug could only be filled halfway.

She also learned songs and the discipline of singing. Her voice naturally tended toward high notes, but she was trained by Verlie to reach even higher scales and to sustain the notes longer. Most of the songs she learned from Verlie were simple ones. Many were songs to help speed the days' weaving. Yet she was also asked to practice odd combinations of sound, and she was taught to breathe with strength and care.

The women of Trost helped her with the frustrations of her blindness as best they could. Parella, whom Snow-Eyes found abrupt and often long-winded, showed her how to thread a needle by touch and how to spin; Verlie, who seemed exasperated by Snow-Eye's clumsiness, taught practical things, like how to fill a glass without overtopping it. Lammar, who seemed to Snow-Eyes much more patient than any of the other servitors, despite what Beya had said, taught her how to dip the huge, ceremonial floorcandles. The candles delighted Snow-Eyes because they were so large, as tall as a child and as thick as a small tree.

Yet even though she shared her daily work with the women, rising when they did at cock-crow and dining with them at each meal, she seldom spoke to them and never dared to ask them questions because Beya had strictly forbidden her to. "Lammar, Verlie and Parella do not have the time," Beya would say, "to answer idle questions. They are too deeply involved in service to the Mother; their silence and their solitude ought not be disturbed."

"But what does service to Trost mean?" the girl asked her mother one day. She and Beya were sitting in Beya's bedroom. It was a large room, crescent-shaped and joined by one of the villa's strange clicking doors to the room that Snow-Eyes had been given. Each morning, after the day's baking was done and before the day's weaving began, Snow-Eyes would meet with her mother in this room for lessons. Much of the time was spent listening to Beya tell tales about Trost—tales that always showed the Lake Mother's benevolence. Soon, the girl grew to hate the morning lessons, because she seldom had the opportunity to ask about the things that puzzled her. Whenever she did ask, Beya would counter the query with one of her own, or ignore the question altogether.

So, even though Snow-Eyes learned that every one of Trost's servitors had once lived in a Kield or in the countryside—Lammar had been born in a valley of Kheon Kield, Parella and Verlie had come from Adeo—she never found out how long the women had been with Trost. Though she learned that each had suffered blindness, she never discovered how many seasons had passed before their sight was returned.

She was told once that usually only four servitors lived on the island at any given time; this number, and the number of their tasks, was set by ancient design. When the eldest of the four had become old and was ready to give up her duties to another, a wandering servitor was called back, and the youngest was free to leave the island—to wander, to love, to help the people of the Kields and to bear a new daughter, a child or children gifted deep with insight, one of whom—or perhaps more, depending on the circumstances—would one day learn service to Trost. Beya said that she herself had left the island the very day that Zonel, the eldest before Lammar, had gone to the Sea of Sansel's Net with Trost. From time to time, particularly of late, there had been gaps in the round of servitors, and during those times no wishes could be answered, no hopes fulfilled and things often went sour and sad for the people of Gueame; from time to time, two sisters might serve at once, to make up for the gap—as Zonel and Lammar had, being sisters. And when Zonel had gone, Lammar had taken up her sister's duties— and Verlie had taken up Lammar's and Parella had taken up Verlie's and Beya had stepped into Parella's place—just as Snow-Eyes would someday take up Giolla's duties. Giolla was the youngest of them now, said Beya, and she was wandering the land of Gueame, carrying a child who might, per-haps, take Snow-Eyes's place when the time came.

Yet no matter how often she asked, Snow-Eyes was never told how far Beya had gone on her youthful travels, nor of how she had met Paudan. Nor did Snow-Eyes learn if every child born to the wandering servitor might be gifted enough to learn service to Trost or if she had other siblings besides Edan and Edarra. Once she asked her mother, "Why do we put bread and water on the windowsill?" and got the answer, "For Trost's child." Snow-Eyes felt that she did learn—but never enough.

Yet she persisted in asking her questions.

On this particular day, she said, "What does service mean?"

"It means giving and obeying." Beya took a brush to the girl's hair and began to braid it. "We are servitors, as I have said before. Most of the bread we bake is sent to those who wish for bread. The cloth we weave is for those who do not have enough cloth. Any offerings I might be given by grateful Kieldeans while I travel are given in turn to those who need more than I. For ourselves, our lives have been given over wholly to the Mother. She offers us, for our obedience, the power to step into our dreams, the power to see our dreams and to become them—as I made you and me into the silverns that day."

Snow-Eyes held herself very still and breathed softly; she was surprised to have gotten so much of an answer. Turning her head a little, she ventured to ask, "When will you teach me?"

"When you are ready," said Beya. She pulled the brush through her daughter's hair in three quick strokes. "Then you will learn."

"Ready? What do you mean?"

"I have told you before, child. Have you not heard? When you are ready to vow your life to Trost. On that day you will begin to see."

"But what ... what if I choose not to vow?"

"You will give of yourself. For us, there is really no other choice. Do you want to be blind all your life?"

Snow-Eyes shook her head vehemently so that the brush bristles tore her hair and she heard the brush clatter on the floor. She ran from Beya into her own room, pulled the door shut behind her, then paced up and down before the open window, up and down, thinking. I do want my sight back . . . I want to go home, too. Why won't the Lake Mother give me a choice? Why must I vow to her? How can she be so cruel to me? Snow-Eyes slapped her hands together in frustration and turned around, bumping against a table. Where is Trost? Why does she hide from me? She must be hiding somewhere in this villa—she must be! Waiting and watching me. I've got to find her and go to her and ask—Snow-Eyes stopped pacing. What would she ask of Trost, if she could find her? For sight? The Lake Mother would demand a vow; Beya had said so. Was it possible to ask for freedom? That would probably mean giving up a chance for the insight that Beya had spoken of—it might even mean giving up the chance to have her plain sight returned. If Trost had not given her first four servitors a choice about suffering the blindness, why would she grant Snow-Eyes any favors at all? If Beya and Lammar and Verlie and Parella had each suffered the tears of Trost gladly and had made their vow gladly, without asking for more, then Snow-Eyes was sure that Trost would not look upon her request for both power and freedom with favor.

Snow-Eyes groped her way to the bed and lay down. How can anyone love the Lake Mother? she wondered. Why did Paudan pretend that she was kind? She is cruel.

The door to her bedroom clicked open, and Snow-Eyes propped herself up on her elbows.

"It is time to begin weaving," said Beya. "Let me finish with your hair."

The girl stood and loosened the half-braided locks, combing her hair with her fingers. "I will wear it free today," she said.

Beya took hold of her daughter's arm and led her out into the corridor. Together they headed for the loom chamber, which was near the kitchen. As they went, Snow-Eyes hoped that the work that day would not seem so endless. She often despaired during the hours of thread and shuttle, longing for the afternoon so that she might leave the chamber to do the cleaning and candle-making.

When she had been a little girl, she had loved weaving. She had loved the odor of the wools and the fine textures of the flowing cloth that grew under her hands. She had liked to work with Edan at the loom and to watch the emergence of the bright design. But in the Lake Mother's villa, weaving only made her sad. Instead of sitting behind the shuttle, she was made to spin and spin and spin. She was never allowed to work the spun thread into whole cloth. Weaving, it seemed, belonged to the servitors, and until she had made her vow and received her insight, she would not be a weaver, only a spinner.

Beya and Snow-Eyes passed down the staircase to the kitchen with its warm odor of bread baking, and from there into the loom chamber. Beya murmured greetings as Snow-Eyes sat in her chair and picked up her spindle. She fingered the stone whorl that weighted the spindle, as the looms around her began to chatter from the movements of shuttle across weft and woof.

And the women chanted:

Red for thy blood and the matters of thy soul;
Yellow for the sun and the dance of thy memory;
Blue for the wise and thy wisdom's flowering;
Indigo for the night and the hue of thy dying.
White for the weaver, who gathers them all.

The chant was sad and lovely to Snow-Eyes. The women sang it in four parts, their voices as clear as the bells of seasonchange. The music was woven between them just as the cloth was woven, and the shuttles seemed to sing to the beat of the women's song.

Snow-Eyes felt utterly alone. Though she knew the words and melody, she was forbidden to sing during the weaving because she was not yet a servitor. Listening to the chant and loom chatter, her heart grew tight and sore. She sat and spun and tried to swallow back that soreness, lest she cry aloud. She wished to stand up, to throw away the tedious spinning, to wrest the shuttle from Beya's hand. She wanted to tear Beya's weft, tangle the woof, rip the pattern off the loom.

But she did not.

And as the seasons passed, Snow-Eyes learned to live from task to task and from day to day. She did what she was told to do, and she learned what she could from Beya. Always she listened for a sign that Trost might be present. Alone, she waited—waited for Beya to tell her she was ready to start learning about the insight; waited for her soul to wish to vow obedience to Trost; waited, though she felt trapped, like some angry, baleful creature.

Little by little, she grew accustomed to her blindness. She learned that her ears, nose and fingertips were excellent and trustworthy companions. She began to feel less confusion and more curiosity, until at last, one spring day after the weaving was done and before the midday meal was served, she decided to take a chance and do a bit of exploration, as she had once explored the shadows in the flat-roofed home across the lake.

She left the kitchen and told herself as she mounted the stairs, "Now, Snow-Eyes, you will only go a little way. Not too far from the kitchen. You don't want to be lost again. But a little way on your own . . ."

She went, telling herself over and over that she would not walk so far as to lose the sound of the servitors' voices in the kitchen. She reached the top of the staircase, holding her breath. She took a step and then another and made it halfway down the hall before she turned and scurried back to the kitchen and safety. She had not gone very far, indeed, but the spell of fear she had lived under since her first day in the villa had been shattered. She would not get lost. The next morning she went farther—all the way down the hall to her room.

☆

Afterward, she explored the villa whenever she might slip away from Beya's scrutiny. Since she could only see with the tips of her fingers, what she discovered about the villa was fragmentary and confusing. It was a puzzle with pieces lost. The kitchen, her own bedroom and Beya's and the cold, circular weaving chamber, these she came to know from ceiling to floor. Still, all the rest remained a mystery. According to one of Beya's tales, the villa had been built in four separate sections, called "nidules." These nidules were attached to one another by long, subterranean passages and by the large, half-buried rooms such as the kitchen. Each of the nidules had six levels, and in the last level at the top of all, hung a bell of season-change, housed in a roof pavilion. There were no stairs in the nidules; instead, the floors of the halls inclined, going up and up, around and around the circular levels until they reached a trapdoor that led to the bell pavilion. Snow-Eyes pictured the whole villa as a collection of four, huge seashells that had been sunk into the earth by a giant's hand.

Though she tried to remember each nidule and all of their different circular or crescent chambers, she could only keep a memory of three of them in her head. The fourth, no matter when she visited it, was never the same. Indeed, she began to suspect that the fourth nidule's rooms rearranged themselves merely to confuse her; or else someone kept moving the furniture and things— beds and floor-candles, chamberpots and chairs—from room to room. Unless they moved themselves, creeping behind her back on stubby legs.

This changefulness made exploration a rigorous challenge and decidedly frustrating. If the one nidule could rearrange its furniture, someday the whole villa might decide to shift! She made up her mind that anything could happen, anything at all, and she feared to fall through a new-made trapdoor or to walk into a room that changed itself into a closet and to have the door lock or vanish behind her.

Yet even so, as the days went by, the strangeness of her life with the servitors melted away. She took delight in some of the things that had once frightened her—things such as the doors that clicked open at a touch or the stairless nidule hallways. She became eager to feel everything, and by feeling their texture to see them: the thick, knurled wool that the women wove, or the patterns of wood grain in a lathed table leg or the odd, dancing designs inscribed upon the nidule's walls. Sometimes she found herself tickled into giggles by the fourth nidule's abrupt and changeful nature. Nothing that happened there surprised her; she did not even startle the day she discovered all the boxes in the whole villa cluttered together in the smallest room atop the nidule, each box filled with fragile, tiny seashells like the ones Paudan had kept in his workroom.

She grew even bolder. One by one she explored the countenances of the women of Trost. Beya's face was long and firm, narrow and bony. Her cheeks were high and planed flat; her eyes curved upward toward her temples. Lammar's face was long also but her skin was as soft as chick's down. Her eyes were round and small. Verlie had a wide mouth that smiled often, while Parella was angular with a high forehead and full lips.

Snow-Eyes began to find these faces familiar, and with familiarity came warm affection. By the time the third winter chilled the window glass and made the girl huddle under three blankets at night, she felt that she knew the villa well and that the women cared for her in their own silent way. She even felt at home, especially during those winter evenings that she spent sitting over a pot of tea shared among the women and listening to them speak about the wishes they had heard that day or about their dreams.

It was not on a winter evening, however, but on a winter day, as she was going up to her room, that Snow-Eyes found she was no longer heart-sore or as lonely as she had been as a child. She stopped in the hall near her room and thought, Where has my anger gone? Am I ready to vow? She searched her soul; deep inside it, buried by time, she felt the anger hiding. It had not gone. It had become a cold passion, burning cold, the kind of anger that could wait, inexorable, forever, and it was coiled around one, unanswered question: why had Trost taken her away from her home and given her no choice but to serve? Why?

Snow-Eyes fisted her hands until they shook. If only Trost would show herself! If only Beya would soften her manner and give her daughter a little care—instead, Beya always found fault.

The girl leaned toward the wall to steady herself, but although she leaned and leaned far, there was no wall to touch. She walked forward inch by inch down the hall until her fingertips brushed the cold stone once again. She inched her way back and found the place where the wall stopped; a doorway stood where drapery usually hung. She searched for the rug and found it looped back upon itself, tied to a hook inside the entrance by a silken rope.

What is this? she thought. A room? A closet? She stepped into it—and fell. She cried out—a wordless yelp as she slid down, rapping her elbow sharply as she tried to grab hold of something, anything. Down, down a flight of stairs she went, having missed the first step. At the bottom she landed flat on the floor.

A whispering, rustling sound greeted her.

Shakily, without moving, she said, "Beya?"

"Beyabeyabeya." Her own voice made a hollow answer. Snow-Eyes sat up. She could feel a bruise starting on her cheek. She said, "Who—"

"Whowhowho," said the echo.

She stood and whispered, "Can it be?"

"Bebebe."

After all this time, she was afraid to believe that she had finally found it: the echoing room where she had first met Lammar, Verlie and Parella.

Overjoyed, she hurried around the room's perimeter despite the queer, moaning echoes that scurried after her. She searched by hand and with her ears for the narrow, dank corridor that would lead her to the huge door and from there, outside. She yearned for the forest, for the sun, for home. If she could find the door, she would be free, blind perhaps, but free to find her way to the island's shore. If she did reach the shore, maybe a fisher would hear her calls and row her across the lake—perhaps the fisher might even be Edan!

She searched the room once. Twice. Then, slowly, a third time.

She found no door, no hall.

Snow-Eyes stood still and thought, There

has to be a door. I know, I remember it! Confused and heartsick, she walked toward the middle of the strange room. If she could not find the way to the sun and the forest, she would explore the room instead. So she walked along beside the wall, listening to the moans and rustled echoes, tapping one foot before her as a guide. Around and around the room she went, narrowing her revolutions until suddenly she came to a part of the floor that seemed soft under her feet. She halted. A rug? She got down on her knees onto—what?

Plants, leaves, earth and the smell of the damp soil . . . she laughed and the room laughed with her. A garden! She had found an atrium garden, like the one in her home across Lake Wyessa. Snow-Eyes tilted her head back and felt the weak sunshine on her face. The roof, she thought, must be open to the sky. She could feel a draught of winter air. She crawled further across the interior forest. Her cheeks were brushed by the flexing boughs of finger-thin trees and by lacy, fringed leaves. The earth was muddy and smelled tangy, as the air had smelled under Trost's trees that never shed their leaves.

Crawling in the earth and underbrush, Snow-Eyes felt lighthearted as she went along, happy in her discovery. After a few moments she sat back and took deep breaths of the fresh, frost-touched air. She leaned forward and bumped against something large and rough—larger and rougher than any of the garden's miniature trees could be. She touched the thing with one hand.

It was a stone. A rock. Wide, round and squat. Though it was not fancifully carved, she knew what it *had* to be . . .

"A wishing stone . . ."

"Wishingstonewishingstonestone."

Snow-Eyes crawled backward to the edge of the garden. There she knelt and thought, That must be Trost's own wishing stone. Must be—could it? She rubbed her hands against the material of her trousers meditatively. "Should I make a wish?" she asked herself. "Dare I?"

After a while she got up and walked back into the heart of the garden. She put out her hand. Her fingertips brushed the sharp edges of the top of the stone. She caught her breath, clenched her hand and did not move. She could not make herself touch that stone. She wanted to make a wish; she wanted to ask Trost for her sight and for the chance to go home.

But . . .

What would happen when Beya heard this wish? After all, the women of Trost could hear all the wishes in the world. What would Beya do?

And if Trost granted her desire, would

Snow-Eyes have to give up all of the gift of insight? Would it all be taken from her before she even knew just what the power of insight entailed?

Exactly what did she want?

Chastened by her indecision and the cold, Snow-Eyes stuck her hands in her sleeves and went away, went back upstairs to her room.

☆

After her discovery of the Lake Mother's wishing stone, Snow-Eyes became very quiet. She did not ask Beya any more questions. She stopped crying in the middle of the night. She went to visit the flowers and tiny trees and the sunshine of the atrium garden often; she would sit near the stone, among the gentle fronds, with her back against gnarled roots and would think. She was trying to decide what it was that she truly wanted.

In her musings, she began to regard the Mother's wishing stone as a fog-bound boat's anchor, firmly rooted in the heart of the house. While staircases might hide and doors disappear, while the nidule's furnishings might dance secretly from room to room, the wishing stone and its garden—now that she had found them—were always at the bottom of the stairs behind the drapery. It was a place set apart from the rest of the villa, unconnected with the day-to-day work and unchanging except for the seasonal life of the garden's plants.

She did not tell the servitors about finding the stone. She supposed that they might not have wanted her to know about it because, since that first day, they had never shown her the room or the garden. And so it became her secret, her own private place to go and be alone and to wonder: if a wish made upon a wishing stone had taken her into the Lake Mother's villa, why wouldn't a wish to leave take her home again? Was she willing to take the risk of losing her sight forever? Was she willing to give up the chance to learn about the insight?

There were days when she was sure in her heart that she was ready and that all she needed to do was ask Trost, who was bound to answer any wish made upon the wishing stone.

And yet Beya had said time and time again that Snow-Eyes had no choice but to remain on the island and serve. What would happen if she asked Trost for something she was not supposed to want?

What shall I do? she wondered as she sat in the miniature forest with her legs stuck out before her and a fern tickling her cheek. Wishes are tricky things. Before I wish for anything, I must be sure I know my own heart's desire.

7

Lies

AN OWL HOOTED.

Snow-Eyes sat up in bed. A steady breeze blew in through her open window, a breeze that was sweet with the breath of sunstars.

"Whoo-whoo!"

The girl pushed her blanket down to her ankles and got out of bed, being careful to duck her head so that she would not hit it on the low roof. Touching the wall with two fingers, she guided herself to the open window. The sill was waist-height to her. She put her elbows on it and leaned out.

"Whoo-whoo!"

The owl sounded as if it had perched close. She listened for a rustle of leaves and another hoot. Then, an odd thought made her draw back from the window a bit. She remembered the wishing stone in her faraway home, and she remembered how she had not-dreamt of the owl carved within it—of how she had not-dreamt the stone owl into life.

She wondered if she were not-dreaming now. Could that hoot-cry be the voice of the stone owl, come to her window because she was sorrowing, come to carry her home?

"Whoo-whoo!"

Snow-Eyes extended her hand slowly out into the night wind. She felt the breeze. Concentrating, she pictured the black stone owl. She pictured it sitting in the forest across from Trost's villa, teetering on the bowed, sweeping branch of a tree. The branch swayed. The dark creature sprang from its perch and glided in a long, low swoop silently down to her open window. Her hand trembled. Pinions grazed the tips of her fingers.

This soft touch of feathers made her start—she had called the owl! It was there! She could nearly see it, a blacker shadow than the night of her eyes' blindness. Suddenly, though, she felt small and vulnerable. She tried to pull her hand inside, away from the creature, and talons closed on her arm. The grip crushed her muscle, and the strong, cold claws tore her skin. The bird yanked Snow-Eyes against the wall and half out the window, and she shrieked and wrenched her arm away from—

Nothing.

Snow-Eyes hugged her hand to her stomach, expecting ragged slashes, blood, blood. She sobbed. Bending over from the pain, she turned her back on the night wind and oh-so-gently felt the wounded arm over, wincing.

But her skin was whole. She touched her wrist again and massaged her forearm. There was no blood. She stood straight. She was unscathed; yet she could still feel the crush of the bird's power and the slicing sharp talons. She turned back around to the window.

"What are you looking for?"

Snow-Eyes glanced toward the sound of the voice and said, "Beya?"

"I thought I heard a cry in here. Were you dreaming?"

"Yes." Snow-Eyes reached out to let the breeze cool her sweaty hands and face. "There was an owl. I thought I heard an owl."

"Is that what you are looking for, there out the window?"

"Looking . . . I cannot look for anything."

Beya let her daughter's bitterness pass without a word. She sat down on the bed, her nightclothes whispering against the floor as she moved. The bed frame creaked. She said, "Tell me. What happened?"

Snow-Eyes leaned her forearms on the wide sill once again, resting her chin on her hands. "Home," she said. "I was looking for home."

"Ah, child, that is the past. There is nothing for you in the past."

Snow-Eyes did not answer.

And so Beya said, "Your sister sold you for the price of the villa."

"I know it. She is still my sister."

"I am your mother."

"Mother." The girl turned away from the gusting wind and the forest that she could only see in her mind. She remembered the little boy she had met in the Kield hall: he had been so proud of his mother and so sorrowful to hear that she did not have one. She thought of Paudan, who had told her that the Lake Mother was kind. She thought of all that she had believed a mother to be and she said, "You did not care for me when I was little, you did not stay to be with me, you were not there! Why should I care if you are my mother? You stole me from my sister—"

"No—"

"Yes! By offering her a gift she had to accept. You took away my eyesight—"

"Because—" interrupted Beya.

"You teach me nothing! And . . . and I don't want to learn anything from you, now." Snow-Eyes found herself shaking. She had never spoken so deep a truth before, to anyone.

"Are you sure?" murmured Beya. "Can you really think, child, that you have not learned much from me already? Do you imagine that you've taken nothing from me—from all of us?"

Snow-Eyes slid down along the wall's curve and sat on the rug. She thought of the four women of Trost and tried to picture their faces though she had never seen them. She tried to think of what she might have learned from each . . .

. . . small, sharp Parella, who spoke as if something were chasing the words out of her mouth, rushed, loud, running up an octave and then down again, the words all mumbled together. Snow-Eyes needed to listen closely and curb her impatience with Parella, if she wished to speak with her . . .

. . . tall, round-faced Verlie, who shouted her words when she was pleased and sang queer little songs off key to keep herself amused. Verlie, who seemed convinced that only she knew how hard she worked and how many hours she spent making the bread rise and the tea brew. Snow-Eyes had learned to be quiet around Verlie and to refrain from telling her how foolish she sounded, because then Verlie would be hurt . . .

. . . and silent Lammar, who might pass hours without a word and yet whose ruminations were never simple. She was kind to Snow-Eyes, by far the kindest; she was the only one of the servitors who listened to Snow-Eyes's complaints with patience. Abruptly the girl said, "Patience."

Beya sighed and said, "You have learned some, yes."

"But that isn't what you promised!"

"No. No, of course not. How can you dare to ask for so precious a gift from me, or from Trost, without offering me a readiness to give? You are selfish—and a child. You are not ready for the insight."

Snow-Eyes stood up. Her face felt hot and her mouth dry. Outside, a cock crowed, reminding her of the old chanticleer who strutted in silly, self-possessed splendor about the yard of her home. His staring, yellow eyes had seemed brainless with greed, as if, to himself, in his narrow cock's mind, he was a Drake Villae, a ruler of many. But he had never soared beyond the yard. Snow-Eyes thought she preferred the owl, now. Dark and dangerous, at least it was free. She said, "I don't want to learn anything from you. Even when I am ready."

"Oh, come, don't be sullen."

Snow-Eyes shook her head. Her single braid swung to and fro.

"Would you not like to know how to make the furniture move from room to room?" asked Beya.

The girl caught her breath—so the furniture in the nidule did move! She had not imagined it! Nevertheless, despite this discovery, she let out her breath and said, "No-o-o . . ."

"Or how to hear wishes and answer them?"

"No. No." Snow-Eyes hid her face in her arms.

"Or even how to glide on the wind like your nightowl dream?"

Snow-Eyes whimpered, but she continued to shake her head.

"Child!" Beya stood up. She lowered her voice and said, "Would you not like to see Paudan again? To make him come from your dreams into life? Together, you and I could bring him back to us—oh, my little one, I would teach you all of this, if only you desired it. You have to want to learn my ways from me, you have to promise yourself to Trost. Why is it so hard?"

Snow-Eyes clung to the windowsill. Her heart beat fast, faster; she could feel it thumping in her chest as she leaned against the smooth wall. When she spoke at last, her voice was gruff. "I . . . I want to see Paudan. To learn the insight, I do. But . . . but you hurt him. I don't want to be like you—dark, hurtful and alone. Maybe I am selfish. But I will not become a servitor, if it means being like you."

Beya said nothing. Her hurried, running footsteps went across the room and out the door. It shut behind her.

Snow-Eyes pressed herself against the curving wall and let out her breath again. The room was quiet. No owl hooted, and the cock was silent. She was alone. She sat down on the rug, crossed her legs and thought, I said it. I said "no" to her. Snow-Eyes breathed her heart into a stiller beat. She shed no tears.

☆

"Could I learn to become like you? Could you teach me?" said Snow-Eyes to Lammar. They were in the kitchen. The sun had not yet risen, and neither had any of the other servitors. As the girl kneaded blade-seed dough, the old woman shaped flat loaves from the batch they had made yesterday.

Snow-Eyes was sleepy. Her eyes would not stay open, and she kept rubbing them and yawning, powdering her cheeks with flour. She had not been able to either doze or crawl back into bed after Beya had left her room, so she had dressed and wandered down to the kitchen, where she had found Lammar awake and making the bread. As she worked alongside the older woman, she decided that, if she had to become a servitor, then she wanted to learn the insight from Lammar. If she had to become a daughter of Trost, then she would pattern herself on this woman, not on Beya. If she had, indeed, been selfish to wish for freedom and the gift of insight, then she would learn the art of giving from the one who had given her the most. Gathering her courage, she asked, "Could I be like you?"

Lammar put down the grater she had been using. She said, "Nutmeg is best when it is freshly ground. To grind away a whole nut, to put the nut-dust in a box in the dark, this I don't like. Beya does it, but the flavor is lost." She paused. "What am I like?"

"You are . . ." said Snow-Eyes. "You—" She dug her fingers into the stiff lump of dough and pounded the bread against the table. "You listen to wishes . . ." she said lamely.

"Yes. We all do. Listen. Answer them, when the time comes."

"That's not . . . It's too simple."

"Is it? Answering wishes is not a simple task."

"I know, but—" Frustrated, Snow-Eyes squeezed the bread dough harder. Finally she said, "Do you move the chairs and tables and boxes and things in the nidules from chamber to chamber each day?"

"Me? No. Parella does that. She is native to Adeo Kield and fond of games, as most people in Adeo are. Stability bores her. Here—stop. Enough. Kneading it more will stiffen the dough, and we will have loaves akin to stones."

"Parella moves—"

"Yes, yes. For amusement. It annoys, but one gets fond of her inventiveness. I know that it is particularly hard, without your sight, to be taxed with some of her foolishness. Beya had a terrible time with all of Parella's games. She has told you, I'm sure. Here, that's enough nutmeg." Lammar took the bowl off the table. "Did you ask Beya—"

"No." Snow-Eyes wiped her hands on a towel that she had tucked into her trouser's waist. "I haven't asked her about the furniture. I . . . don't ask her much of anything, anymore."

"Why?"

"I don't want to."

"But she is your mother, Amarra!"

"Yes," said Snow-Eyes. "She has told me so."

Lammar walked across the room and slid a tray of the flat loaves into the oven. Radiant heat touched Snow-Eyes's face as the oven was opened. Lammar said, "Did you hear the rooster singing this morn? Sang his old heart out." She paused, then said, "You are full of questions, Amarra—I can feel them all tangled in your throat. Have you not asked your mother even one of them?"

The girl whispered, "My name is Snow-Eyes."

"Yes . . . your childhood name is Snow-Eyes." Lammar touched the girl's shoulder. "Why don't you ask your mother questions?"

"I have. She does not answer. And now . . . I'd rather ask you."

When Lammar said nothing to this, Snow-Eyes did not know what to do. She wondered if the old woman did not wish to answer her questions either; or perhaps she was angry, as Beya had said she would be.

But Lammar said gently, "I see. What is it that you would ask me?"

"Could—could I be like you, could I move the chairs around and—"

"Yes, you might. But, whatever for? You are not Parella. You are not me." Lammar collected the mixing bowls, stacking them noisily. She poured water into a trough and said, "Come, help me clean these."

"If I learned to be like you—"

"Amarra, you are already *like* me—you are a woman, you are my daughter's daughter, you are a child of Trost. You cannot help but be like me. What you ought to learn is how to be yourself."

"Daughter's daughter?" said Snow-Eyes. "What do you mean?"

Lammar took in her breath sharply. "Surely—! Beya is my child. You are my grandchild. This is the way it has always been, for the daughters of Trost. Verlie is Parella's mother."

Snow-Eyes bit the inside of her mouth to keep from shouting. She had known—in her heart, she had known, yet Beya had never spoken of Lammar as her mother, only as a servitor. And how much more had Beya kept hidden? What else? A thousand questions oppressed Snow-Eyes at once, wanting to be asked; finally, she said, "And if I did become a servitor, as you are, could I really see Paudan again?"

Lammar pulled her hands out of the dishwater and took Snow-Eyes gently by the wrists. "What did you say?"

"If I wished to, as a servitor of Trost, could I see Paudan again? Not just in dreams, I mean, could I bring him back from the Sea?"

Lammar tightened her grip. "Your father has died," she said quietly but forcefully.

"Yes, but Beya said—"

"No." Lammar released the girl's wrists and walked away from the dish trough. She clapped her hands, then called aloud, "Beya!"

Snow-Eyes backed toward the stairs, her face flushing. She had never heard Lammar's voice betray so much anger.

Beya answered, "What is it?"

Now Snow-Eyes was confused. Where was her mother? She had heard Beya's voice, but had not heard her enter the kitchen. Where could she be? Her voice sounded both near and far, both in the room and beyond it, as if she were speaking through a closed door.

"Come here," said Lammar sternly. "Wake thyself from thine insight and come here."

A few moments passed in silence. Snow-Eyes eased toward the staircase—if there was going to be an angry argument, she did not want to be a part of it.

A whiff of honeysuckle and a slight whisper of skirts against the floor told the girl that her mother had come as called.

Beya said, "You sound upset, Lammar."

"I am. Did you tell Amarra that she might see her father again—that she might call him back from the Sea?"

There was silence from Beya in answer.

Snow-Eyes whispered, "You said—"

"I know what I said!" Beya turned around and took a few steps toward her daughter. Frightened by the vehemence in Beya's tone, the girl edged further away and nearer to the stairs.

"Beya," said Lammar. "Leave her alone. You've been scaring this child silly, I think. How is it that I find your daughter ignorant of so many things? How is it that I find her unwilling to ask you, her mother, questions? How is it that I find her wishing to learn lessons from me and not from you?"

Another voice drifted into the kitchen before Beya could answer. "What are you arguing about now? I cannot listen to you and attend to my dreams at the same time—"

"Go back to sleep, Verlie," snapped Beya.

"What we are doing does not concern you. Stay out of it."

"I will not." Verlie's voice became clearer and more distinct. "I will not." She hurried down the stairs, her wooden heels clattering against the stone. She said, "Lammar?"

"Beya has told Amarra that she might see her father again—see him outside of her dreams. To bring him back from the Sea."

"What? We can't—"

"How do you know?" cried Beya in a high voice. "Trost can return to us from the Sea, during the ceremonies. How do you know—"

"It isn't right," said Verlie. "Trost has strength beyond all people."

"So do we. As her daughters, we have power. And the tales say that our ancestors could—"

"—do many a thing that we cannot," said Lammar. "And should not. When Trost first walked among us, we knew more of her ways. We have lost some of her gifts, child, you know that. You have been studying her lore and her powers long—surely you know how much we have lost."

Two heartstrokes of silence went by. Then Beya murmured, "You have never cared how much I loved him."

Lammar sighed. "You could have stayed with your Paudan. It was your choice to remain here, to spend most of your time here. You knew he could never come to the island, and you chose not to stay with him, for his lifetime, but to follow the deeper reaches of the insight instead. You chose power and your gifts over your love, and though I know it was not an easy choice, you made it. Just as when you were young and I asked you if you would accept Trost's tears—"

"Accept?" said Snow-Eyes. "You asked Beya if she would accept the dark? Do you mean I ought to have had a choice about the tears?"

"Choice?" said Lammar. A deep note of worry ran through the fiber of her voice. "Of course, every daughter has the choice."

Beya said quickly, "No—"

Verlie said, "Oh, Beya!"

"Liar!" cried Snow-Eyes. She turned and sprinted up the stairs, up and up, up to get away, to hide, to find a place to sit and hide and think. Everything had changed and was different, just as the nidule's geography could change. In an instant, a few words had changed all of her perceptions, as if someone had taken the picture of the Lake Mother that Paudan had painted and hung it upside down. She had not been asked to accept her blindness; it had been thrust upon her—why? Why had Beya lied? And why had Beya told Snow-Eyes that she had had no choice but to leave Paudan all those years ago? Snow-Eyes shook her head as if she might shake the truth loose inside it. She could understand now why her mother had forbidden her to ask the other servitors questions—for fear that the hidden truth would be revealed. As it was, now.

Snow-Eyes reached the top of the stairs; she stumbled and banged her knees on the floor. She bit her hand to keep back a cry of pain, got up and felt her way along the wall. Her palm ached with the teethmarks she had made, but she continued running down the hall, away from Beya, her fingertips brushing the smooth stone lightly as a guide until she grabbed the tassled selvage of the hanging drapery. There she stood still, caught her breath, and listened: The women were in the kitchen. They had not come after her. She could hear them down there, arguing. She looped up the heavy drapery and stepped down the stair, letting the rug flap in place behind her, its tassels sweeping the floor and flicking against her ankles. The air was cool. She smelled new-turned earth warmed in the sun.

As she stood on the stairs, in the dark, her heart speeding and her breath echoing loud around her, she thought, Perhaps I do have the choice to wish for my eyesight and my freedom, after all. Perhaps Beya lied to me about that, too. Perhaps it is not Trost who is cruel . . .

"No," cried an inward, terrified voice. The voice was her own. "Trost will forbid you—you must vow. Remember what Beya told you—"

"I don't know," she said aloud. She took a step back and put her hands on either wall, bracing herself as if she were about to fall. "What shall I do?"

And then she remembered what Lammar had told her: "You ought to learn to be yourself."

Snow-Eyes sat down on the top stair, pulled the end of her shirttail under her and thought. Grandmother. The word was strange to her, yet it filled her with warmth. She wished she had known earlier who Lammar was. But in a strange way, she *had* known. Not in words, but in the way she felt toward Lammar and in the way she had begun to feel toward all the women of Trost, even her mother whom she did not understand. They were her family.

She frowned and clasped her hands, hunching her shoulders. Who was Snow-Eyes? What did she want? To go and hide in her room as a child would? No. To see again? Yes. To go home? Yes, but to have also the insight that Beya had promised her. These were her heart's desires. She would have to ask Trost. And if Trost forbade her to go home, she would . . . she would choose to be a servitor. She would make the vow.

Snow-Eyes stood up and took a step down. She had surprised herself in discovering that she would choose the power of insight over the wish to go home. But as she took another step down, she knew why she would choose dreams. Not because she was selfish, as Beya had charged her, but because dreaming was her gift. She had been born with the beginnings of that special gift of insight. It would be wrong to deny it, as Paudan had tried to do for her.

But it would be wrong also to deny that she wanted to go home. It would be lying. She could never vow her life honestly to Trost without first asking her heart's desire.

As Snow-Eyes descended the staircase, she imagined herself to be as bold and as unafraid as the huntress owl that had come to her window in the night. She thought, I have waited too long. I have waited for the answers to arrive unbidden, when what I needed to do was seek them out. I needed to look inside myself. I want to use the gift of my dream-sight. I want to go home. Perhaps I may not be granted both. But I will ask.

As she touched the chamber floor with her booted toes and stepped into the room, the sound of her footsteps whispered up the stairwell behind her. Standing quite still, with her arms resting at her sides, she listened intently to the echoes, because in the echoes she heard voices . . . other voices in other rooms, rooms far away; but the voices were caught here, in this room where unfinished dreams and unspoken desires haunted the air. All the wishing stones in the land of Gueame were but shadows of this one stone. All the hopes spoken to those shadow-stones found voice here, in the Lake Mother's villa.

Whispers of despair, disharmonious, tugged at Snow-Eyes and demanded from her some sort of response. Shrieking and sighing, the voices swirled around her. Faint murmurs fluttered wildly, like a surfeit of night-borne moths, singly insubstantial but lent a cloying weight by their multitude. She could hear them all for what they were: the ghosts of impossible wishes waiting to be filled by the Lake Mother. She knew, too, that the voices had always been in the room—she simply had not heard anything before this moment beyond the din of her own soul's confusion.

Fresh air blew in from above, and a scattering of rain pattered down. The interior forest's mulch smelled rank and rich. She crossed into the garden and walked through the silky, abundant fronds and past stiff blades. She reached out. Her hand smacked stone. She ran her tongue over her skinned knuckles and hesitated.

Then, she put both hands on top of the stone and bowed her head. The rough rock felt warm, warmer than her hands, which had become chilled with sitting in the stairwell. Her head felt light and her skinned knuckles throbbed. Sighing with the tension inside her, she hoisted herself on top of the rock and sat there with her legs dangling. She closed her blind eyes, and just as a weaver might order a thousand ragged threads, she meshed her hopes into a single, simple wish . . .

"I want to be myself, as I am. To know myself."

Echoes parroted her words, but she ignored the audible shadows and climbed off the stone to get down on her knees beside it. She held on to it with both hands until the sharp edges needled her palms. She touched her forehead to its warm surface.

The room became quiet around her. She emptied her mind of everything but the silence and her hope. Then she opened her eyes.

Darkness: a smooth, lymphic, nacreous black, a star-shot night. She blinked away clouding, sticky tears and stood. The black ice receded, and she knew that she was looking upon a facet of the wishing stone. She bent down. In the polished concavity she saw a blurred, oval face: a dark woman with canted, silver eyes.

Is that me? she thought. But my eyes, what has happened to them? They are like

Beya's ... She reached out to touch the face in the stone, but the reflection of her hand grew to cover the woman in the stone. She stepped back.

"Amarra?"

For the first time in her life, Snow-Eyes responded to the name her father and her mother had chosen for her. She turned around so quickly she nearly lost her balance.

The four women of Trost stood huddled at the foot of the staircase together. One of them had called her by her name, but she had been so distracted by the image of herself in the wishing stone that she did not know which. She wanted to smile at them all, to laugh high, to caper around like a maddened, frisking creature, full of joy. Embarrassed, she glanced down and saw again, for the first time in many, many seasons, the lush, proud-flesh red of just-blown sunstars; the curved lancets of yellow, newborn blade and the brooding green of its matured growth; the rarefied blue patches embroidered at the garden's edge by cockleshells; a white snowstar, five-pointed and premature, and the black, coruscate beauty of the stone. Delicate, feathery red leaves shivered in a breeze. She looked up. The nidule's roof—she could see now that the whispering room was, in fact, an entire and separate nidule—vaulted overhead. The walls were white and spiraled up to a circular,

open window; the walls then spiraled down
and off into four, scallop alcoves. Each alcove was frescoed with a curious image,
one of which glittered, flecked with gold, in
a pool of sunlight.

She wanted to rejoice. The garden reached
out to her soul and shook it with beauty.
She wanted to cry out; but she did not
because the four faces behind her, all so
solemn, checked her fierce exultation. Though
she had never seen the women before, she
knew them: that one, her white skin wrinkled and her silver eyes almost lost in fold-
ings, that one was Lammar. Verlie, behind
Lammar, as thin as a hunter's arrow, her
black skin smooth and her hair gone as
silver as her eyes, she had her arm around
little Parella, dun-skinned with dun hair;
her round face was startingly similar to
Verlie's, and her silver eyes were dark-circled
and thus seemed to be bruised.

And Beya. Beya, whom the girl had seen
once before, who stood now a bit apart from
the others. She seemed to have aged not at
all from the woman her daughter remembered. Even though her straight stream of
black hair was touched with a strand of
white here and there, she was still young.
The daughter stared at her mother, and a
thought came to her: You are not a child
any more, Amarra. How can your mother
be so young?

Beya said, "Do you see me, child?"

Amarra hesitated a moment. Then she nodded.

"No . . . I'm not ready!" said Beya. She stepped back, and then turned around. "No."

Lammar hobbled after her. She put her arm around the younger woman's waist. Beya sobbed and whispered, "I'm not ready. It's too soon." She laid her head on her mother's shoulder. "I'm not ready to take my final vows."

"Ah, child," murmured Lammar. "We all grow old too soon."

Amarra stood and watched her mother and her grandmother with the joy she felt for her returned sight hugged inside her like a secret candle's midnight glimmering. Briefly, for a moment then, she saw what Beya saw: herself, a woman now, young and strong and unfolding, beginning a flight that Beya had already flown. This knowledge made her feel a tug of sadness in response to her mother's grief. She had a swift memory of Paudan's aging face, his crooked hands and the white hairs upon them that had told her he was old.

Leaving the garden's embrace, Amarra walked toward the daughters of Trost, her gaze upon Beya's back. For a moment she glanced up at Lammar, whose bright eyes expressed encouragement. Emboldened, she said, "Mother?"

Beya stiffened. She raised herself from Lammar's arms slowly and turned.

Amarra started to say something more—but what? She closed her mouth and chose to smile instead, though she knew that the smile would be imbued with the joy of her sight returned, the joy that would not be tethered to solemnity nor tempered by grief.

Beya did not speak. She did not smile. But she touched her daughter's face briefly and rested her hand on her daughter's shoulder.

8

A Ceremony

A CHITTERING of minute tree-frog voices and the drizzle of an afternoon rain gave the wishing stone room an ambience of expectancy. Amarra stared at the dark and dappled gray sky and glimpsed a brief streak of lightning. Thunder rolled.

Lammar scooped a lick of black, gummy paint out of an open pot with her finger. Holding Amarra's chin firmly with her free hand she said, "Quiet yourself." Then she began to rub the paint down Amarra's temple, past her eye and over her flat cheekbone to her chin. As her face was painted, the young woman examined her grandmother to see what the painting would look like when it was done.

Two jagged blue lines followed the contours of Lammar's skull, making her face seem sharper and thinner than it was truly. Blue paint on her eyelids enlarged her silver eyes and made their glance cold. It was a fierce glance. Yet, at the very heart of it, Amarra saw a spark: fire. As if to echo this hidden warmth, Lammar's hair was curly and red-brown, hardly faded by gray. Her fingertips were dry against Amarra's cheek. As the second black streak was painted on the girl's face, she shifted her gaze, without moving her head, to see what the other servitors were doing.

Verlie stood to the right of the wishing stone with her hands clasped loosely before her and her gaze on the white floor. Her cheeks were painted with jagged lines also, but the color of the lines was yellow.

Parella and Beya stood to the left of the stone. They were speaking to one another. Amarra could not hear what they said. Beya appeared calm. The grieving she had done and the tears she had shed several days before were gone. Her cheeks were made pallid by white streaks.

Parella wore red paint. Each of the women was dressed in a dolman dyed the color of her facial streaks. Over this dolman, each wore a black, floor-length robe. Amarra felt uncomfortable in hers. The sweeping flow of the fine-woven garment made her look taller, and as graceful as a slim wand of grass. But Amarra missed her trousers.

Lammar wiped her hands on a soiled scrap of material and put the scrap and paint pot down into a floor niche, where several other pots stood, along with a mortar and a pestle and a collection of dried seeds. She said to her granddaughter, "Beya has dreaded this ceremony, I believe."

"Yes . . . but why? She has told me many times how she loves Trost."

Lammar nodded slowly. "She does . . . still, this ceremony means that she must now use her skills fully, all that she has learned from Parella and all that deep power she gained from studying the insight. It is a large responsibility, and she must give up another measure of her freedom—for with each level of power must come sacrifice and discipline. Making her final vow also means that she is no longer truly the youngest of us—she has not been, of course, since the day Giolla came here to study; but as long as you were still a child, without the benefit of your dream-eyes, and Giolla was not here, Beya felt young and somewhat free to pursue the powers of Trost as she chose. Two days ago, when you opened your dream-eyes and received Trost's gift, she was forced to understand that her daughter was now a servitor. She was forced to know that the time had come for her to make her final promise and to see you begin your own journey. She has wanted you to follow her ways—our ways—and yet I think she has feared it also."

"She kept the truth from me," said Amarra

bitterly. "She told me that I had no choice but to vow myself to Trost. She said that without the vow, I would be forever blind."

Lammar stared at her granddaughter with a puzzled air. "That is the truth," she said.

"But I did not pledge myself, Lammar. I only asked that the Lake Mother accept me as I am. I showed her my heart's desire: to be free to choose, to be myself. I made no promise to serve as you serve. I only promised to be myself and truthful."

Lammar seemed taken aback. She shook her head slowly and said, "Trost favors you."

Amarra bit her lip. She looked at the ground. "The Lake Mother has granted my wish. That is all."

Lammar nodded, but she did not speak.

"And Beya," said the girl, "Beya did not ask me if I would be willing to accept Trost's tears. She said that I had no choice there, either, that I must suffer blindness because I belonged to the Lake Mother."

"Yes ... it was wrong of her. If Verlie or Parella or I had realized that she had taken your sight without your consent and that she had not answered your questions, nor taught you properly ... She tells me now that she thought you were not ready." Lammar shook her head again. "It was wrong of her, very wrong. She should have come to me—or gone to Trost. But I never thought . . . She is my daughter, I never thought she could do such a thing."

"Yet she did—why?"

"Have you asked her, child?" said Lammar gently.

"She will not speak to me," said Amarra quietly. "Even now."

The old woman glanced across the room. The ends of her mouth turned down in a pained expression that was both sad and tolerant. "What I think is that she was afraid you would not accept the tears. She must have feared that you would not want to follow her—and she had already vowed your life to Trost, as we all vow our gifted daughters. Yet she did not know you; she had not been mother to you; she could not be sure that you would still want to follow the ways of Trost, even though you had said, when you were little, that you wished, 'to be like the Lake Mother someday, to have silver earrings and make wishes true.' Do you remember?" Lammar smiled.

"I remember."

"Well, Beya knew that she had been mistaken to leave you to grow up without her. Perhaps she also feared that Paudan had told terrible things about her; I know she desperately hid what she had done from me. All those years, while she studied the insight, she told Verlie, Parella and I that she was visiting with you as often as her studies would allow. That she was teaching you. We did not press her. You were her daughter. What reason did we have to doubt her? As I said, to have a daughter who will follow us into service, this is one of the pledges we make at our second vowing. Beya wants you to follow. Yet, at the same time, she did not want to have a daughter at all. Seeing you grow up reminded her that she was aging. As you became strong, she would grow old. Can you understand?"

Amarra nodded. She said, "I would have refused the tears. She was right to fear so. But everyone grows old—I know that I will."

Lammar sighed. "Yes, but does it frighten you?"

"A little."

"A little. But it scares my daughter a lot, I think. So, she pretended to herself that you were a child long after she should have seen that you needed her love, not her descipline, her companionship, not her silence. I worry for her." Lammar folded her arms. "She and I have grown apart. We quarrel now nearly all the time. She has not confided in me since she was your age, and she has grown more and more silent, withdrawn. I thought she would grow out of it, in time. I thought that caring for her own child would bring her out of herself. And now ... she does not see that only courage and the willingness to accept change brings wisdom and true power. She believed that you would refuse the tears because she had never taught you what they were for, why they bring blindness. She had not reared you as she was reared, with an understanding of Trost. Then, suddenly, Paudan was near death, and there you were . . . her daughter, full-grown and untaught. She acted, I suspect, out of fear, Amarra."

"Nevertheless, I should have had the choice. And I would have chosen to stay home, with my brother and sister, where I belonged."

"Would you have, truly? Would you have forsaken your childhood dreams and the gift that Trost has given you—without a vow!—so easily? Where do you belong, Amarra?"

Snow-Eyes did not answer. She turned and walked to the other side of the room, past Verlie and over to the eastern alcove. She turned her back to the servitors and to the wishing stone. She stared at the fresco on the alcove wall, but after a few moments she saw, not the painting, but a memory of herself as a little girl in dusty pants. The little girl sat in the front room of her home, pretending to be the Lake Mother.

"Would I have forsaken that child's dreams?" she asked herself. "Have I?" She shook her head. No, she doubted that she could have and knew that she had not.

Blinking away memories, Amarra focused

on the fresco. Over the past several days, she had been busy learning the answers to many of the questions Beya had ignored. From Verlie, she heard the tale of how Trost had built the nidules, patterning the villa after a seashell, so that she and wild Aenan and their child might have a home on the earth. But Death, jealous as always, had come and stolen the child away. Trost and wild Aenan grieved, as did the first four servitors, Trost's handmaidens. They waited season upon season for Death to return the child's soul. They laid bread out and water, to make the soul welcome. They rang the bells of seasonchange so that the soul might not lose his way. Trost wove blankets and blankets and blankets so that the soul might remember what it was to be a child and cold at night. But no soul returned to her from the Sea, and finally, Death came to steal wild Aenan, too. And so Trost lost herself, her mind, for a while. In that time, she made the villa hold the tale of her love and her child's loss on its walls. All the days and all those nights she spent painting the frescoes in the wishing stone room, and when that was done, she decorated the curving walls in every chamber with her sad and shrieking tale, and thus the first language of Gueame was born. The servitors tended to her as she worked birthing the first language, and so she gifted them with her tears, that they might pass on a little of her power.

"One day," said Verlie, finishing the tale, "Death returned. She saw him in her garden, his dark face wet from the everlasting Sea. He held out his hands to her. She no longer saw him as angry or jealous. He was, simply, her brother. And she went to him, then. She went back with her brother to the Sea. Now, it is we who are the Lake Mother; we are Trost."

"Death is a man—Death is the Lake Mother's brother?" said Amarra.

Verlie glanced at the young woman who walked at her side. They were climbing a nidule to one of the roof pavilions, discussing the ceremony that was to be held on the next day, discussing Trost. Verlie made a slow smile. She said, "To me, Death wears the aspect of a man."

"To Beya also. I remember she startled me by calling Death Trost's brother. But Paudan told me that no one knew whether Death was a man or woman; he always called Death the Lake Mother's sister."

"And to you? What aspect does Death wear?"

Amarra stared at her boots as the two women climbed up the hall toward the pavilion. She said, "I have yet to see Death's true face."

"Ah." Verlie stepped up a small ladder

and pushed open the heavy trapdoor. Together she and Amarra climbed through it
onto the roof and into the pavilion.

Amarra gasped. The bell of seasonchange
hung in the center of the pavilion, shining
with a soft yellow glow from the setting
sun. The roof itself was circular and open
on all sides, upheld by six stout columns. A
breeze blew, strong enough to make the bell
moan a bit, as if it were preparing itself to
sing. A pole, suspended by heavy ropes, hung
next to the bell, waiting to be pushed by a
servitor's hand at the season's change.

But Amarra had gasped because of the
expanse below. She could see far and wide;
she saw all the lands of Woodmill and
beyond, almost to the borders of Kheon
where the mountains rose. On one side of
the pavilion, she saw the black gates of
Woodmill Kield and all the small villas clus-
tered near it. On another side of the pavilion, she could see the sparkle of the White
Sea, and the thin snake of the Middlemost
as it meandered across the green and yellow land. Yet, because it was a circle, the
pavilion had no sides and so she could see
all of this, her homeland, at once. It made
her giddy.

Verlie leaned against a pillar and smiled.
She said, "Shall I tell you more of Trost?"

Amarra turned away from the brilliant,

sun-touched view, and said, "It's so beautiful. But it looks so small, from here."

At this Verlie laughed. "The world is small. Have you not felt how little we are, you and I and the lake and the land, when the stars are clear in an evening's sky? Have you not felt the touch of another, larger world, when you dream?" Suddenly, Verlie's face became still and shadowed. The sun dropped below the horizon. She said, "Let me finish with my tale, before the eve. Death had held tightly to his nephew's soul and had taken wild Aenan, too. He thought he could bring his sister back to the Sea in this way. He thought that he would be triumphant when she came to him. But he was not, and in the end he went to her not as an enemy, not as a jealous, hurtful power, but as her brother. And that is why she went with him. She has not left us, of course, not altogether—who do you think makes the spring come? Who is it that melts the ices of winter? It is Trost; for she vowed to her servitors when she left this earth that Death would never reign entire. Those first four servitors, those whom she called her daughters—"

"You! You—"

"Not us, Amarra. Our ancestresses, our mothers' mothers' mothers'."

"Yes, I know, but you are Trost's daughters in the same way they were, is this so?"

"Yes." Verlie frowned. "It is a difficult

thing to understand Trost. She is here, with us, always, and yet she is not here. She is the spring, she is the flower of the field. We are a part of her and we share her powers, and yet she is not diminished by our sharing and is within us as much as we are within her. We are her daughters particular— and yet all of Gueame is her child. Her children. As you and I are part of each other's life, she is a part of life. We care about one another. Trost cares about us all."

"Have you seen Trost? I have never seen her, not even when she granted that I might have my sight."

Verlie leaned down and pulled the trap-door open. She said, "You shall meet her during the ceremony for Beya. Tomorrow. Come now, the lesson is over. We must make supper. And then, you must sleep. Since you have received your dream-eyes, Beya must vow; and it will be a long day for the both of you—and me, too!"

"Verlie? Did . . . did Trost let her first servitors choose the tears? Or did she make them blind without asking them?"

"Of course they had a choice." Verlie held out her hand. "Come."

Amarra sighed, remembering how relieved she had felt when Verlie had said, "Of course." Standing in the alcove, she looked up again at the painting on the wall before her. As part of her lessons she had been instructed to study each of the four paintings in the wishing stone's room. The frescoes were ancient and recounted the tale of Trost's life, inscribed as they were with words of the first language. Verlie told Amarra that only the servitors could read the language, although the Wise Ebsters in Mossdon Kield could still speak it.

So Amarra had studied the frescoes, beginning with the one in the east alcove where she stood now. In the painting, Trost was dressed as Amarra was dressed for the ceremony, all in black. She carried an infant in her arms. Under her bare feet, a full sun rose. The animals hidden in the grove of intertwining vines and buds and tender leaves were all asleep—the tadpole in its pool, the owlet in a tree, a calf and a lamb on the grass. The inscription looked like:

EAST

ᗰᔑ ʔ~ʔᒪ~ᘚᓍᒪ~ᓴᙢᒪᙢ ᗰᔑ ʔ~ʔᒪ~ᘚᓍᒪᒕᐟᐁ~ᑲᖆ

chea ses nifunet ono; chea ses nifunet scino

Amarra had not yet learned to read the first language. Verlie told her that the words said, "Black is one. Black is none."

The southern alcove showed Trost in a

red dolman. The sun at her feet was also red. She carried an armful of flowers. All around her the garden was in bloom and the creatures hid in the radiant patches. The ewe with the bullock hid behind sunstars, the tadpole, which now sprouted tiny legs on either side of its tail, flitted among the water lilies. The owl slept in the budding trees.

The inscription here read:

SOUTH

C (7~ 7ʊʊ~ʌʌ τ 7~ 7ʊ0ʋ~ᴽ

ba segyye chea ses ruscet

which meant, "Red for the blood."

In the western alcove, Trost sat on the ground, dressed in yellow. Her hair was shorter than it had been in the eastern or southern painting. The flowers she had carried were strewn on the ground, dying. The sun and blue moon were both at her feet and her arms were spread wide, as if she were expecting a child to run to her. The ewe lay beside her and the bullock stood. The frog climbed out of the pool. The owl watched the woman with open, yellow eyes and the inscription read:

WEST

ᴍᴛ?~ᔑ()~6?= (ᒐᵐᔑᒪⵠ(~ᔑ

chea set demspanot fulet

which meant, "Memory's yellow."

Trost wore blue in the northern alcove and she was seated upon a tree stump. Her hair was white, and the sun was not to be seen, leaving the moon only at her feet. The ewe suckled a lamb and the bull stood alone. The pool teemed with new-hatched tadpoles. The owl flew above Trost, bearing away a ribbon with the inscription:

NORTH

Ͻⵠ(ᒐ~?ⵠᎭ~??~ᒪ

gwanes woes sef

meaning, "Blue and wisdom."

Amarra walked from the northern fresco back toward the east as Verlie began to light the floorcandles in the silver sconces that stood in each alcove. When all the candles were lit, she closed her hands on a drop of flame that she had been carrying upon her palm, extinguishing the dreamlight.

Beya walked to the eastern alcove; Parella

to the south. Amarra knew that the time to begin had come. She took her place in front of the wishing stone as she had been instructed. She hoped that she would remember everything the servitors had taught her about the ceremony, though pieces of it kept slipping from her mind as she stood and fingered the sleeves of her dolman.

Lammar began the singing. Verlie had told Amarra that it was for this song that her voice had been trained; it was a lament, said to have been written by Trost so that all would remember the awful day when her child was stolen away. The servitors would sing it in two languages—first in the tongue of the southern Kieldings, which they all spoke, and then in the first language, the Lake Mother's own.

Lammar sang the opening verse. Then Verlie began, repeating the words. As Amarra stood and listened, she hoped she would be able to follow her thread of the song and prayed that she would not become entangled in another's. She hoped, too, that she would be able to intone the first language properly. Parella began; Amarra swallowed. Her throat was too dry. She swallowed again and thought, Please, let me remember all the words. She heard Beya finishing the first verse and opened her mouth:

Oh, where have you gone,
my darkling child?
Have you followed the silvern
down to the sea?
I have gone nowhere,
O my mother,
I have not followed the silvern,
nor followed the sea.

My eyes cannot see you,
my darkling child.
You have fled from my side,
oh, where can you be?
I am here, O my mother,
come touch me now, come run with me.
My face is cool, in the evening's shade.
My face is warm, in the morning's sun.

My eyes do not see you,
my darkling child.
But I hear your voice in the night.
You are as warm as the sunshine,
of a new day's waking.
You are as cool as a nighttime shade.

The room became curiously darker, and
the wishing stone seemed to glisten. Amarra
caught her breath at the end of the last
verse; there was a full beat of silence before
Lammar began to sing in the Lake Mother's

tongue. It sounded low and mournful and sighing, like wind,

    Hĕîh lōĕdĕn-sĕn kōnōànî

    nîftōn pōmȧ

Amarra swayed. The humming and the rise and fall of the song soothed her, drawing her toward sleep but at the same time holding her to wakefulness. The singing went on and on, each voice melding to the whole, yet remaining separate.

Amarra kept her gaze on the wishing stone, as she had been told to do. Rapt, cast gentle on twilight waters, floating between dream and waking, she saw without surprise that the black, glassy facets of the stone were becoming light. The whole stone pearled to gray. The gray became clearer and clearer, leaching from a smoky fog to transparency, until the rock was indistinguishable from the rainwater that fell upon it.

Woven into the song's music came the shrieking, sighing, sorrowful voices that spoke of wishes made upon innumerable wishing stones in all the villas of every Kield. Amarra shivered. A gust of wind blew rain into her eyes, but she did not take her gaze off the garden.

A face appeared inside the stone. For a moment, Amarra thought she was looking at herself. But soon she knew it was not so, that the face was no reflection but rather it was in the heart of the stone, a woman's face—

Trost.

Amarra's voice faltered an instant as she realized whose silver eyes were those in the stone. Trost faded momentarily; she mouthed words, but there was no sound beyond the unintelligible whispering of lost wishes and the humming of the servitors' song. Amarra thought the Lake Mother looked worried. Her thick brows were drawn forward and her gaze darted from side to side.

Then Trost nodded, as if in answer to a question. Her face shrank, shrank, shrank so small that Amarra thought it was going to vanish. But no—instead of vanishing, the whole woman now appeared in the stone: a tiny delicate figure, as small as the figurines that Paudan had once carved for his children. The woman stood inside the light, suspended; then, the image divided, splitting apart from the center like a bloom bursting open all at once so that there were five small figures, five imp-Trosts—quintuplets where a moment before there had only been one. The light of the stone grew stronger, spilling over the boundaries of its form.

And the images walked out of the light, one to the south, one to the west, one to the north and two to the east. Each trailed a filament of yellow brilliance.

Amarra wanted to run. Her skin prickled

and her hair snapped eerily, as if it had caught fire from the stone, a white shower of sparks that did not burn. She glanced at Lammar, who stood without fear in the northern alcove, and took courage from her grandmother's calm face.

One of the tiny figures of Trost approached her; she was touched by its light, and the floor seemed to tilt under her and the room spin. Amarra fell, or thought she was falling, and then the room, the garden, the light, everything was gone.

She found herself sitting on the bank of a stream. The sun was warm on her face; a spring breeze made the ash trees wave their boughs. The sky was cloudless, and black lake gillians cried to mate. Amarra stood. Not far from her, a group of women sat, talking. To her surprise, she felt as if she knew them. They all seemed quite familiar, but in a very disturbing way because she did not know their names. They were dressed in the style of the servitors of Trost, dolman and robe, yet their clothes seemed well worn, almost shabby, certainly not fit for a ceremony. Where had Verlie, Parella, Beya and Lammar gone? Where was this place?

Perplexed, she walked toward the stream. Her body felt sluggish and slow, as if she had only just wakened from a midday sleep. She glanced at the other women. They, too, had stood. They looked about them as if they had lost something. Amarra nearly stopped to walk back over to them. But when she hesitated, so did they. She stared. One by one, the women folded over, bending at the waist, and in a queer motion, sprang into the air, changing into owls, great, dark owls with shining eyes . . .

Amarra ran to the edge of the creek and made ready to jump across if she could. But the owls, silent, flew overhead, their wings shadowing black crosses on the waters. She looked down at the trickle of the clear stream over smooth, brown rocks and the yellow rushes edging the banks and the gillians feeding in a deep pool, and strangely she was reminded of the Middlemost.

But, she thought, it can't be . . . it is too narrow, too small. She looked . . .

She screamed.

In the deep pool among the gillians, floating face down and much too still, a little boy . . .

Amarra half-slid, half-scrambled over the muddy bank, stumbling into the water after him. Her robe tore and weighted her as it got soaked, making her clumsy and too slow, too slow. The gillians cawed their annoyance as she staggered among them, and they rose to the air like a funnel of dark smoke. She lifted the child's body, her first child, Aenan's child, her little son . . .

Amarra caught a sobbing breath and

looked up. The dream was gone—the sky full of gillian-smoke, the drowned child, all gone. She knew that she had shared Trost's sorrow; briefly, she had become Trost; briefly she had lived a past made present and had taken on the Lake Mother's loss as her own. Now it was done, as was the lament she had been singing. The stone in the center of the nidule's garden no longer held an image.

Into the silence, someone said, "Daughter, what do you ask?"

Amarra flinched. Was Trost speaking to her again?

"Mother," said Beya, "I ask to be with you, as you are always with me. I pledge to you myself and I ask you to accept me forever. This is what I promised when a child, this is what I promise again, now, as a woman grown. I am a daughter of Trost."

"Daughter, what have you seen?"

This time, Amarra knew the questioning voice was Lammar's.

Beya answered, "I have seen my Mother's pain. I have felt my Mother's sorrow. I know the way of giving is hard." She faltered, but only for a minute. "I am ready."

"And Daughter, having offered us the gift of your life, what is it that you wish?"

"I wish—" Beya took a deep, sighing breath. "I wish to have my Paudan once again. With my daughter's help, we can call him back from the Sea. As my Mother once called to her son."

"No . . ." whispered Parella.

Amarra froze. The stone's shimmering gray dulled and fogged again. Trost appeared within it for a moment; her face lengthened, twisted, smeared and was lost as the gray light molded itself into another, different face. A hearty gust of rain and wind made the candlelight in the alcoves flicker and dim. The moaning of lost wishes returned, grew loud. Vague shadows moved amongst the garden's growth, flitting in and out leaves and flowers like tiny birds.

Amarra took a step closer to the stone. She knew that she should not do as Beya had asked. She knew that she should not help her mother bring Paudan back from Death's abode. She could feel the wrongness of the wish tug at her heart. But her own wish, to see Paudan again, tugged back. She stared, without blinking, into the writhing fog that was the stone. And the face there began to form more clearly, coming out of the darkness and turning slowly toward her.

Paudan.

He appeared a young man, then an old man; his face grew and shrank, child to adult, adult to child. His expression was not calm, not as it had been in all of Amarra's dreams, but pained. He seemed to be calling out; his mouth was open . . . but his eyes were closed. The smoky darkness clung to him in a thousand tiny webbings of black. The webbing pulled at his flesh and held him tight, disfiguring him.

Amarra took another step forward, and her foot touched the earth in the garden. If only she could reach him, if only she could tear aside the blackness and pull him to her . . .

He moved his head back and forth. The fog grew denser. It covered his forehead and masked his eyes.

She took another step, brushing aside the one blossomed snowstar of the garden. Its white petals broke away from the stem and dropped to the ground.

A soft, wheedling man's voice called her name in a husky whisper. "Snow-Eyes. Dear child, come to me."

Was it a woman's voice? Was it Trost? Or Paudan?

"Snow-Eyes, dear child. Come here, come to me, and there will be no more worry. Let me take care of you . . ." A young man appeared in the stone. Amarra could not see his face clearly at first, but his eyes shone silver, like her own. He leaned forward and held out his arms to her, his wide, flat hands cupped. His movements were graceful, his attitude infinitely gentle. He turned so that she could see his nakedness and the strength in his long, muscled legs. "Let me hold you," he whispered. She still could not see his face clearly.

Amarra closed her eyes and turned to one side. She did not want to listen to him anymore, afraid she would be unable to resist his offering. Though she understood that he who spoke was Death, his seduction was as strong as an ocean tide. She folded her arms over her heart and said, "Not yet, not yet. You have already taken Snow-Eyes, she is not here. I am Amarra."

"No!" It was Beya. She ran forward. "Paudan!"

Lammar cried out too and dashed after her child with more speed and strength than Amarra had thought possible. The candlelight in the room shivered and went out.

But the darkness was no stranger to the servitors of Trost. Amarra could hear her mother and grandmother struggling in the garden. Her ears served her as well as her eyes might have, if there had been light. She hurried across the earth to where her mother stood and locked her arms around the woman's waist. Pulling hard, she dragged herself and Beya to the ground. A branch cracked and broke under them as they fell.

The last glimmer of gray pearlight on the stone died instantly.

Beya sobbed. She curled into a ball, hid her head in her arms and did not move.

Amarra lay where she fell also, until two pinpricks of dream-light winked near her. Verlie, Parella and Lammar stood beside the black stone; a raindrop of fire sat unburning in two of the women's palms. Lammar knelt next to her daughter while Amarra got to her feet.

Beya sat up slowly. Her face-paint was smeared into wet patches on her cheeks. She looked to the wishing stone. It stood as it had before the ceremony, black-faceted and quiet, surrounded by flowers.

Beya said, "Paudan was here."

Lammar clapped her hand over the tongue of light she carried, and it went out with a small puff of smoke. She shook Beya gently by the arm. "How could you? How could you risk Amarra's life in that way?"

Beya looked confused. "Risk?" she said as she pulled her arm away from her mother's grasp. "She is young and strong with insight. Did you see him? Together, Amarra and I might have cheated Death."

"No," said Amarra. She brushed dirt off her palms. "No, Death called me to him. I would have taken Paudan's place in the Sea—a life for a life."

Beya shook her head.

Lammar said, "Have you not learned, have you not seen that no one, not even we, may live without Death? Trost called to her son, yes. But he never came. He never came!"

189

"Beya," said Verlie. She handed the flame that she carried to Parella. Her voice was deep and forceful. "Beya, if Trost ever held the power to cheat Death, it is a power lost. And better so. Did she not, even she, join her brother, at long last? Trost knew that life is precious, but it is only one state of being. Death is another."

"Paudan," murmured Beya. "He once sought for life everlasting. He did not want to leave the earth for the Sea."

"But Paudan quit his searching, didn't he. He knew it was wrong."

"Did he?" said Beya. Her silver eyes spoke a challenge. "How can you know? He loved me. And I want him back."

"You had the chance to live with him," said Verlie cruelly. She stepped behind Amarra and put her hands on the younger woman's shoulders. "You made your decision, Beya, when you left your daughter and her father, when you left and never visited. I'm tired of your complaints." Her tone was icy. "Lammar may forgive you. But I don't know that your daughter should."

Verlie's hands tightened on Amarra's shoulders. And Amarra felt shaken by unshed tears. Her forehead was chill with drying sweat. She said to her mother, "Did you want me to trade my life for Paudan's? Did you know that Death would take me in Paudan's stead?"

Beya stared at her daughter and said nothing. But Amarra could hear an answer in the silence, an answer that made her colder than any winter's frost. She wrenched away from Verlie's grip and ran past the wishing stone to the stairs.

Beya cried out, "I don't know—I didn't know! Can't you see? I loved him, I knew him, I wanted him . . ."

And I am a stranger, no one, thought Amarra as she hastened up the stairs to the hall above. Her dolman's hem caught on her boot heel and she ripped the cloth. Pulling up the torn edge and gathering the black robe in one hand, she ran on.

☆

In the predawn darkness, the kitchen was cold and empty. Amarra sat on a high stool at the counter where she was wont each morning to roll bread dough into blade-seed loaves. She had made herself tea and was staring out the round window, watching the sun rise. The teapot steamed. Beside her hand, on the counter, lay a satchel. Several of the flat loaves were wedged into it, along with a sack of roots and a block of dark yellow cheese.

"Amarra?"

She turned around on the stool. Parella came into the kitchen from the stairwell.

Her face was drained of color, and she did not look awake yet. Her braided hair was fuzzy, the braids loosened and tangled. She yawned, walked over to the counter and said through a yawn, "You are up and about early this day." She reached for the teapot. "May I?"

Amarra nodded. She said, "I couldn't sleep. Woke up in the middle of the night."

Parella stared at the open satchel for a moment and then poured the tea. She said quietly, "You are leaving."

"Yes."

"Already?"

Amarra got down off the stool and looked out the window again. She was surprised at how cold it seemed out there—almost as if it were winter, instead of spring. She said, "I need to leave. I can't stay here anymore." She closed the flap of her satchel and tied the bag shut, knotting the leather thongs.

Parella sipped her tea. "I think—I think you are choosing to go too soon. You have not yet learned—"

"I know!" said Amarra roughly. "Why do you think I could not sleep? I've been trying to decide, trying to know what Trost wants of me. I must go."

Parella twisted the ends of her dark blonde braid and tilted her head. "It is Beya."

Amarra glanced sidelong at the servitor and sighed. She nodded.

Parella said, "Your mother didn't mean to hurt you; she's confused, she misses Paudan—misses him more than she has been willing to allow. I can understand that. When I first left my love and our children—what, only a short time ago . . ." She stopped. The expression on her face grew distant and pained. Then she said, "Now, my daughter has wandered the lands of Gueame, as I did, as Trost has bidden her. Someday she will come back to us, someday she will leave her lover and her child. Stay with us, Amarra. Stay until Giolla comes home. Your mother does not mean to hurt you."

"But Beya has already hurt me—too much. She wanted me to give up my life . . ." Amarra found her throat dry with the same fear that she had felt when Death had called her to him, so sweetly.

"Where will you go?" said Parella. "It is the custom for a servitor to choose a place to go, before she leaves." She frowned. "And you must speak again with Lammar. You are free to leave; you are the youngest of us and you ought to wander as we have all done. But speak with your grandmother, please. She may feel you are not ready."

"I'm going," said Amarra. "I am going home."

"Home? Your first home? But everything will be changed! It will not be—"

"I know."

"And still you wish. . . ?" Parella finished off her tea. "Stay with us, I beg of you."

"No. She must not," said Lammar.

Amarra and Parella turned around. Lammar had seated herself on the staircase. "It is time for Amarra to go."

Parella's silver eyes widened, and she raised her brows. "The girl cannot be her own teacher—how? She has been granted the insight. She has the power. But her mother has not taught her how to use it well."

"I will not stay where I am not wanted!" cried Amarra sharply.

Parella swung around to stare at Amarra. The woman's dark face grew darker under the weight of her frown. She said, "Do you have no heart, child? Can you not feel the love we all bear you? Can you say such a thing before your grandmother? You ought to be ashamed."

Amarra flinched and turned her head aside so that her tears would not be seen, and she whispered, "I am not loved by my mother. Show me the door, Parella. Show me the door to the outside because I wish to go home." She hitched the satchel up onto her shoulder.

"Lammar," said Parella. "We can't let her—"

"Show the door," said the old woman.

"She will learn. She will learn from Trost. It is time. I've already called Giolla home."

Amarra glanced swiftly at her grandmother. Lammar did not smile, but the look on her face comforted the girl and dried her tears. Hurriedly she stepped across the kitchen and knelt to hug her grandmother and lay her head in the old woman's ample lap.

Lammar brushed back her granddaughter's dark hair. She leaned over and kissed the girl's temple.

"Do you understand?" murmured Amarra.

"Yes, love." She nodded. "And no. I would prefer you to stay. For myself. But you can't."

"No."

"Trost will watch over you—I see it. She will be with you, inside you. Look for her handiwork in the ways of the world."

"Grandmother." Amarra opened her eyes. The old woman's face, heavy, soft and finely wrinkled, was close, almost too close.

Lammar made a pout like a little child and said, "Go now."

"I'll come back."

"Someday. When it is right."

Amarra sat up. She hugged Lammar once more, tightly, bracing her chin on the old woman's shoulder, closing her eyes and breathing in the musky odor that was Lammar. Then she stood and looked to Parella.

Parella washed her teacup methodically

and turned it upside down on the counter to dry before she gestured toward the staircase, ready to go. Together, the two women left Lammar and the sun-warmed kitchen and threaded their way to the wishing stone's nidule. Amarra did not glance behind her as they traversed the curving hall, past the swinging, tasseled drapery and down the stairs. She did not glance back until they had passed the wishing stone, and only then did she turn her head swiftly. She was surprised to find that she felt no regret. She would not serve the Lake Mother in the same way that the other women did, but she knew she was still a servitor: she had been given the insight, and somehow she would learn, learn to use it well.

Parella stopped in front of the east alcove's fresco. She touched the painted child's face on the wall, and it slid back, as the valve of a snail's shell might. A dank, dark passage was revealed. Amarra's heart leapt. There it is! she thought. There is the door, and the path—

". . . home to us at any time," Parella was saying. "Wish to us or dream to us, and we shall answer you. And please—" her voice cracked. "Take care."

Amarra broke from her own thoughts and took both Parella's hands in her own. She squeezed them gently, and though she was smiling, she could feel tears rising once again, and so she hurried away, walking with a firm step away from the villa, away from the hidden garden of Trost, away from the mother who did not love her and toward the forest outside. She did not look back this time, and as she hastened toward it, the huge wooden door that marked the end of the passage swung open for her.

9

The Owl

THE FALLING SNOW made the flat-roofed villa all but invisible. Only the red-painted shutters and the high door with its hammered iron hinges marked the place out from an untouched field of white. Amarra labored up the icy road toward the red shutters, struggling over the fast-growing drifts with the aid of a walking stick. She cursed the sudden storm. It was so odd. Why did the snow fall at the beginning of spring? She remembered the beauteous sunstars unfurled in Trost's garden, and she was glad that they were protected by the nidule from this strange, late frost.

After she had left Parella and Lammar, Snow-Eyes had walked bravely down the same passage Beya had taken her on her first day there, in Trost's home. The passage took her outdoors, to the great stone staircase and to the fragrant woods and thence to the lakeside. As she made her way to Lake Wyessa, it began to snow. In fact, the moment she stepped outside, she noticed the chill and the cutting wind. It puzzled her and hurried her steps, for she wished to get home, to see Edan and Edarra again and tell them all that had happened to her.

As she reached the shore of Trost's island, she found a coracle, painted in blue, beached as if waiting for her, waiting to take her across. She smiled and laughed because she knew somehow that Lammar had put it there for her! Accepting the gift, she rowed herself across the water, as the snow fell silently all around.

Now, approaching her old home, she looked for some sign of habitation. A tiny curl of smoke scrolled above the front room's chimney. That was all. The shutters were closed tight. Everything, including the villa itself, seemed to have fallen asleep.

She reached the door and shook clumps of wet snow from her boots. The front stoop was worn; great cracks fissured the stone. She stretched on tiptoes, pulled back the clapper and let it fall to. The sound of the knock echoed inside the house. Her heart skipped. She glanced from side to side and then leaned her walking stick against the white-washed wall. The red paint on the shutters was chipped and peeling away from the wood underneath. She twisted the sleeve of her black, quilted jacket until faint footsteps sounded on the other side of the door. All the scenes of her imagined homecomings raced across her mind and then raced away. She stood empty, waiting.

The door opened on a tall man with gray hair. He regarded Amarra and frowned. He was taller than she by a head, but his narrow shoulders were bent forward in an everlasting shrug. He said, "Can I help you?"

Amarra was so taken by surprise that she could not think of an answer for the stranger. She wanted to ask, "Who are you?" but was afraid of what he would say. Flustered, she said nothing.

He asked again, "May I help you?"

"I—I've been traveling," she said.

"Yes?" He gazed at her, puzzled. "Here, here, come in out of the wind." He beckoned to her with one thin hand and stepped back into the darkness of the hall.

Amarra hurried across the threshold, glad to see her home again, glad to warm herself. She would ask for this stranger's name as soon as she felt comfortable doing so. She did not wish to be rude. Perhaps he could tell her where her family had gone to—obviously, they had left. She glanced at him again. He seemed quite old to her. She shook her head.

The man closed the door and turned the lock. He said, "You've been traveling?"

"Yes, and I am late reaching Woodmill.

The storm was so sudden! It caught me unprepared and I would ask to spend the night. I fear heavier snow this eve."

He nodded. "You are welcome for the night."

"Thank you." She looked around as her eyes became accustomed to the dark. The hallway was much narrower than she had remembered it. From where she stood, she could just glimpse the atrium garden, frozen and bare. The black, carved wishing stone stood at its center and was polished with a sheathing of ice. She followed the stranger down the passage to the atrium hall, then along the garden's perimeter to the front room. She marveled once again at how abruptly winter had come back to the land.

It must have been a frigid night, she thought, to have put such a thick coat of ice on the wishing stone. During the ceremony of Beya's last vowing, the air had been chilly, but it had been the bracing bite of early spring, not the numbing claws of winter.

The door to the front room creaked as the man opened it. Amarra glanced over her shoulder to where her bedroom had once been. She almost expected to see a little darkling child, dressed in ragged black and barefooted, perched like an owl at the bedroom's door. But there was no one. Though she looked for the child, there was no one and dust lay thick in the corners, undisturbed by bare feet. She smiled at her fancy. Yet, when she turned her back on the hall, she thought she heard the patter of someone running. She glanced back. Nothing; still, somehow she knew that the child-shadow was there, romping. It would always be there.

The man showed her into the front room. Here it was much warmer than in the hall, for which she was grateful. Rubbing her stiffened hands together, she looked avidly about for the things she had remembered with yearning: the mother-of-pearl guitar, the high-backed, stuffed chairs, the two rugs and the painting of the Lake Mother, which she had loved.

But the room was swept clean of the past, except for the threadbare chairs pulled up close to the hearth. It was dark because there were no floorcandles, only the fire's glow. The rugless floor made a hollow sound as she walked over it. In the chair nearest her, Amarra saw the edge of the two brown trouser legs; below those trouser legs, two feet dangled, shod in soft leather shoes. The feet stirred. The person wearing the shoes said, "Who was at the door?"

The old man looked at Amarra and said, "A traveler to Woodmill. She would spend the night. I have told her she might stay."

"Edan, how could you! We don't have a proper place for guests anymore, no food—"

At the sound of her brother's name, Amarra felt her face grow cold, despite the warmth of the hearth's fire. She could not look at him. She did not look. Instead, she managed to walk around to the fireplace, in front of the chairs. Eventually she found the courage to glance at the person sitting in the chair—Edarra?

Thin and bent into a rounded nugget of a woman, she who wore the leather shoes smiled. Her face was lined, but her eyes were bright with frank curiosity. She said, "My brother has offered you hospitality. But we have so little, I am shamed. Things have been hard for us, since I have been so ill. If you do not mind sharing what we have, you are welcome to stay."

"No, I don't mind," whispered Amarra. Her voice had nearly fled altogether. She could not trust it to carry more.

The woman nodded and gestured at the old man. "This is my brother, Edan Nie. I am Edarra. And you?"

"I—I am—" How could she tell her sister? What could she tell her sister? The truth. She had to tell them. "I am Amarra."

The woman edged forward on her chair. "A-Amarra?"

"My name," said Trost's youngest servitor. She sat down beside the hearth with her back to the fire. She was stunned in the presence of her changed family—so changed! —and she feared to say more. How could she continue? What words could be used? She smoothed the pockets on her jacket, trying to think of something to say. Then, suddenly, she remembered what Beya had told her many, many seasons ago, on that first day that she had been on Trost's island. Beya had said: "Time passes differently for us." But Amarra had never thought to ask her mother *how* differently. She frowned at the dusty, faded tiles set into the hearth's mantel. The blue skies of the Alentine Islands had turned a grayish winter white and the green trees had become black with soot. How many seasons have really passed? she wondered. How much of Edan and Edarra's lives? She recalled the days she had lived under Trost's roof and could only find five winters, five summers. How could her brother and sister have become the elderly couple she saw before her now? She glanced over at the two again and thought, I remember them so differently! And I can almost see— She imagined them as they once had been. She thought of the child-shadow she knew was in the hallway, even now, peeking into the front room at that very moment, and she stared at Edan and Edarra. They would be young again. She wished it so.

And they were! Edan sat across from her, straight and tall, auburn-haired. Edarra sat across from her, strong and fair. They were caught in her dream sight as youthful.

I've brought their youth out from my memory of the past ... out from my insight, thought Amarra. She dared not blink. She dared not move for fear of losing them.

But she felt her concentration slipping away. Though she tried to will the vision of her young brother and sister into reality and bring the past to the present, she did not believe that she could; she did not know if it was right. It had been wrong to try to bring Paudan back. Sweating, she blinked and relaxed. The illusion fled; time returned. The two old people were bending toward her with concern.

Disappointment brought sudden tears. Angrily she rubbed her eyes and smoothed the tear tracks from her cheeks. What I saw, she told herself, was only an echo of the past. Just as I can touch Trost's past when I sing that ceremony with the other servitors, so, too can I reach into time and see what has been. Oh! It hurts. It hurts!

"Snow-Eyes?" said Edarra. "Are you. . . ?"

Edan laughed. "Come, Edarra, this woman is not Snow-Eyes." He shifted so that he could look at his guest. "We once had a younger sister who bore your name—Amarra.

She was lost to us, many seasons ago. Through folly."

"Folly?" cried Edarra. "Folly? You wanted to own this villa as much as I did, back then."

"Enough," said Edan. He stood and held out his hand to his guest. "Excuse my sister—"

"Edan Nie, I have told you again and again, I could not argue with the Lake Mother. Besides, I have been dreaming of Snow-Eyes. She will come home . . ."

Edan pushed the worn, raveled chair that he had been sitting in to one side. "Bah!" he said roughly. "I have wished and wished for our little one to return to us. If—"

"I have returned," said Amarra.

No one spoke for some few minutes.

Finally, Edarra whispered, "Snow-Eyes."

"Yes."

"It can't be," said Edan. His voice trailed into silence. His denial wavered. "Snow-Eyes?" While he stared at the floor, Edarra pulled at some loose threads in the chair's arm, nodding to herself over and over.

Again Amarra looked from one face to the other. She folded her hands tightly against her stomach and thought, What else can I say? There are too many years to try to explain, even if I could explain them. She said quietly, "Where did you bury Paudan? I would like to see the grave."

Edan nodded and answered, "We put his ashes out beneath the wishing stone. He had asked me to do that for him, a long time before he became ill."

Amarra stood. She held her hands out to the leaping flames to warm them before she went to the icy atrium.

Suddenly, Edarra clutched at her sister's quilted jacket, tugged and said, "Have you come to punish us?"

Edan stepped near the hearth. "We have suffered enough. Look around you! We have this villa, but nothing else. Nothing!" Fear made his voice harsh. "Time has been hard on us, time and sickness, ever since Paudan died. Edarra could not work, and now I can no longer take care of the land as I once could. We have had to sell our belongings to pay for medicines, to pay the tithe, sold them one by one until there was no life in this villa but our own." He shook his head. "Age can be a cruel thing. If you have re- turned from the Lake Mother to punish us for not seeking you out, then leave, because time has done it for you."

"To see you," said Amarra. She buttoned her jacket and folded her arms, feeling stung. "I came back only to see you, to come home." She started toward the door.

"Stay!" said Edarra. "Please. Don't go."

Edan touched Amarra's shoulder. He said, "Are you really Snow-Eyes?"

"Am I?" she said. Her chin was trembling.

"Oh! Snow-Eyes. Oh, my," he said, clenching his hands. "Oh, my little one." Quickly, tightly, as if she might dart off and vanish, he hugged her to him.

Trembling all over, she bowed her head to rest her cheek in the hollow of his neck. She felt his arms, still strong, surround her. He smoothed her hair as he used to do and put his chin on top of her head. She closed her eyes. She was home.

☆

After a small supper of spiced beans and fish, the two sisters took a walk around the atrium garden together. It had become Edarra's habit to stroll the garden's perimeter each evening before retiring. Edan stayed in the kitchen to clear the supper dishes and to knead the dough for the morrow's bread.

Edarra leaned heavily on her sister as they made their way around the hall. She grasped Amarra's arm. She said, "You are—" Then, she coughed. Her thin body shuddered, and she turned away to hide her face in her hands.

Amarra was frightened. "Here—here," she said. "Edarra?"

The old woman sighed heavily, cleared

her throat, and answered with a query. "You are so young? How so?"

"The Lake Mother—"

"Has she the power to grant youth?"

"I don't know. When I left her home, I thought I had only been gone from you and Edan for a short time."

Edarra laughed. "Short?" she said. "My whole life has passed since you were taken. My whole life." She stopped and pushed open the door to the room that had been Paudan's. She stepped inside and said, "After he was gone, I moved into this room because it is so warm. When we cannot take in enough firewood for the winter, I still have a warm place to be."

Amarra looked around. The room had been changed. The austere, whitewashed walls had been painted eggshell blue, and the bed stood under the windows, blanketed in a red quilt. Opposite the bed stood a straw chair draped with a thick pelt of fur. Edarra eased herself into the chair and covered her knees with a second red blanket.

"My whole life," she said. She picked up a sharp knife and also an ebony figure of an owl that was nearly completed. She began to whittle, and Amarra noticed that the stone floor was littered with black shavings and splinters of ebon.

Amarra said, "May I see it?" She held out her hand for the carving.

Edarra gave it to her and said, "I knew you had not died. I knew you would come back to us."

"I wanted to. For a long time."

"Yes. My whole life."

Amarra felt her face flush. She had no answer for her sister and so, instead of looking for one, she examined the wooden figure that she held. The owl's wings were folded smooth against its back and its round eyes were half-closed. The whittled detail was elaborate and exact, each quill cut delicately, each feather remarkable. Amarra set the creature upright on her palm and thought she would try an experiment. Deliberately, carefully, she rubbed the owl's head.

The little bird blinked; yellow light suffused its irises and its pupils grew instantly enormous. Amarra's hand jumped in surprise, and the owl clattered to the floor.

Edarra picked it up. "Careful," she said. "The wood is hard, but it still might crack." She touched the knife's edge to the creature.

Amarra winced and was about to stop her sister when she saw that the owl was wooden once again.

Edarra said, "Paudan still visits me sometimes."

"Paudan."

"Sometimes. Not often. Each autumn he asks me to plant a sunstar bulb beside the wishing stone. In my dreams." Edarra placed her knife and carving on the table beside her. She leaned back against the fur and closed her eyes.

Amarra waited for her sister to speak again, but soon she heard snoring and so, stealing quietly from the bedroom, she crossed the hall and walked toward the icy wishing stone. There was no sign of sunstars now, out there in the garden. The ground was frozen, barren of anything but snow.

"It is winter," she said to herself as she leaned against a granite column and stared at the wishing stone. She thought, I am young; Edan and Edarra are old. It was spring, yesterday. Today it is winter. Time is all confused. She tugged her jacket close around her breasts, warmed her fingers under her arms and remembered Paudan—not as she had seen him last, but rather as he had been on that night when his beloved, his Beya, had visited him and their only child. She could almost hear Beya singing Trost's lament, which Paudan had loved so. She could almost hear the gentle thrumming of the guitar strings and knew that, if she wished to, she might bring that moment from the past into the present, also.

I hold all time within me, she thought. If only I choose to seek deep inside me . . . insight. She smiled. Dreams. Or not-dreams. This is your gift, Trost, isn't it? She glanced up at the night sky, as if she expected an answer. Through a veil of clouds, the moon shone, a soft and milky blue. I can see what is, I can see what has been, perhaps I might even see what will be—just as I saw that wooden owl share the life of the tree it had once been part of. And I will be the tree and I have been the owl, as I will be ash and the earth someday. Seasons change. We change. We die. But the life is never truly lost.

She rubbed her eyes with the heels of her hands. She was bone tired, more tired than she could ever remember being. Still, she was reluctant to go to bed; reluctant because she was not sure she was ready to sleep in the bedroom she had once shared with Edarra. There would be memories in that room, everywhere. Nevertheless, she took a few steps toward it; Edan was sweeping the floor inside.

"Amarra?" he said.

"I'm here," she replied.

He came to the doorway.

But instead of walking toward him, she stepped onto the garden's path.

"Amarra?"

She held up her hand to tell him wait; then she hurried out to the wishing stone. She stood beside it and looked down at the ice and snow. She knelt. The fierce eyes of the stone owl seemed to regard her as she brushed the snow from the earth to touch the ground where Paudan's ashes lay.

In the morning, after the night's storm had left all its burden of winter upon the land, Amarra woke with the rising sun. She yawned and sat up in the small bed, tucking the faded blue blanket under her arms and staring at the woven pattern of leaves in the wool. It was amusing that she had not outgrown the bed. Lying down again, she closed her eyes and let herself be warmed by the sun.

She was being carried off! She clutched the bedpost as four huge owls prodded her with their hollow beaks. She knew who they were—they were the Lake Mother's first servitors, the ones she had seen at the stream where Trost's child had drowned. They had come to take her; they had invaded her room, breaking through the window, breaking down her door. They had grown thrice their size since she had seen them during the ceremony; they filled the room entirely, suffocating her as she fought to escape. A confusion of dark, shining feathers surrounded her, so soft that they touched her as lightly as a breeze might.

Amarra sat bolt upright, breathing hard. The owls were gone. Wiping a tear from one eye, she got out of bed, straightened the blanket and shook herself awake so that the dream would not take hold of her again. As she dressed, she made herself think of Edan and Edarra. They would have many more questions to ask her this morn. There was much to talk about, much to do.

Out of childhood habit, she made her way to the kitchen. She would cook breakfast for them, all three. But as she passed the atrium garden, she saw someone out there.

Amarra stood stockstill at the edge of the atrium. The someone she saw was Beya. "What do you want?" Amarra said.

Beya sat cross-legged upon the wishing stone, as if it were a cushioned chair. She did not move.

Amarra narrowed her eyes. Was her mother truly there or was this still part of her dreaming? Beya was as transparent as the icicles that had grown upon the twisted columns and roof; she seemed like an ice sculpture, carved atop the stone. Yet her eyes moved, looking about, deep and thick like whorls left in glass by a glassblower's tube. The ice sculpture said, "Come home."

Amarra walked down the garden path. Her boots melted footprints through the thin snow crust. She kept a watch for the mammoth owls because she feared they might be lurking about still, ready to pounce and take her off.

"You must come home," said Beya. "You've been granted the insight. It is not a responsibility to be taken lightly, child. You haven't learned—"

"I know."

"And a vow is binding."

Amarra clenched her teeth to keep them from chattering and said mildly, "I made no vow."

Beya laughed. "So Parella said. Come, don't lie. Trost would never grant you insight without your promise. Look at your eyes, how they shine! You are a servitor."

"Yes. But I made no vow." Amarra folded her arms and glanced up at the sky. High, high overhead, so high as to appear only a black star in the crystal blue, a single bird wheeled. "I am not lying," she said. "I asked Trost for my sight. I asked that I might come home. She granted those wishes."

"Arrogance will lose you your power," said Beya angrily. "You are just a child!"

"Perhaps." Amarra found that she was shaking. Briskly, she chafed her arms for warmth. Maybe I am being stubborn—or foolish, she thought, but she squared her shoulders and asked, "What does Lammar say? What has Trost said? Did she send you after me?"

Beya looked to the ground. "You know as well as I do what Lammar believes. But Trost has yet to speak on this. Mark me, child, she is not pleased. As for your grandmother, she is old. She is mistaken."

"Lammar told me I ought leave. For now."

"Fine! What do you think you will do in the world, untrained and alone?"

"I will follow the dreams that Trost sends. Where she asks me to go, I will go. I wish to stay here, for now, with Edan and Edarra. But later—there is the sea and all the lands beyond it."

Beya's challenging tone changed abruptly as she said, "Please, please, child. Don't be foolish."

"I am not going back with you."

"Paudan's blood," said Beya. She sighed. "Wanderers are unhappy people, lonely people . . ."

"You have wandered."

"And so I know the unhappiness it brings." She touched the owl's head in the stone beneath her and then glanced across the frozen garden to the surrounding hall. The scalloped roof made scalloped, blue-black shadows on the new snow. She said, "Do you remember the first time you saw me?"

Amarra tilted her head. "I remember."

Beya climbed off the stone and leaned against it. She seemed to dissolve momentarily. "I was terrified that night," she said.

"Of what?"

"Of you."

"Me?" Amarra stared at her mother in disbelief.

"Do you remember what you said?"

"I made wishes." A small note of bitter awareness crept into Amarra's voice. "Wishes that have come true."

"And something else. You said something else."

"I . . . I . . . Didn't I tell you to go away?" Amarra shook her head. "No! I didn't mean it. You left because I . . . but I was frightened! You were a stranger, and Paudan seemed so vulnerable before you."

"Vulnerable? Paudan?" Beya laughed. Her laughter was cracked by pieces of silence that fractured the crystal sound. "He was the strongest soul I have ever met. Besides you, my child. Truly. If anyone was vulnerable that evening, it was I. When you commanded me to leave, I glimpsed a flash of your unawakened insight. I was shocked. You were powerful, and your anger hit me as a flame come straight from the sun. It terrified me to see such a thing in so small a child. How could I even begin to tutor that? I fled. In fright, I fled—and, oh, yes, in envy." Beya hugged herself. "For seasons and seasons I ignored my duty to be your teacher and your mother. And also . . . there was Paudan. My Paudan. Though we loved, we also fought. Oh! so much, so much time did we argue over my vows to Trost, my long visits home, my wanderings. I was seeking to understand the depths of the insight, but Paudan wanted me to stay always with him. The more he wanted this, the less I wanted to stay. And even though he was not a young man when I found him, mourning Eda's death, neither was he an old man. Yet I told myself when I finally left both of you that I could not bear to watch him age while I stayed young. I was selfish." Beya caught her breath. "I was wrong. I should have listened to Lammar when she warned me about the gift of youth—"

"Youth?" Amarra took a step forward. "What gift?"

"I told you once. Time passes differently for us."

"Yes, you told me that. Now tell me," said Amarra, "Tell me—how?"

"The tears of Trost. They give us insight, deep and wide. They also give us seasons and seasons of youth, because whenever we sing a full ceremony, whether it is to vow to Trost or to ask her what her will might be, seasons and seasons are lost to us. We enter into the deepest of dreams to touch Trost, we join our four separate insights into one. But if we did not have the gift of youth, we would age too quickly to do the Lake Mother's bidding. Do you understand?

"That night when you saw me for the first time, I had just come from a ceremony. I felt as if I had only been away from Paudan for four seasons. I felt as if I had only left my baby, my Amarra, for a little while. But I had missed all your infancy. Lammar did warn me. I didn't listen, not really. And Paudan seemed suddenly so old!" Beya covered her face with her hands.

"So you left," said Amarra.

"I should have stayed. I know that now. At least until the next ceremony. But it was so cruel, to see Paudan like that, when I had not aged at all! I couldn't bear it." Beya looked up from the shelter of her fingers. "Please," she said. "Come home with me now. There are things I would share with you."

Instead of answering, Amarra said, "I have to know—why did you not give me a choice about the tears of Trost?"

There was empty silence between them. Beya caught her breath and then said, "As your grandmother has said—as I have tried to say, now. I was afraid. I thought that, given time, I would be able to explain to you all that I should have taught you while you were growing up. On that day when I gave you the blindness, you had nothing to make the choice upon. How could I ask you to choose, when you did not know what you were choosing? So I made the decision for you." Beya held out one hand. "You know the beginnings of Trost's gifts now. Come home and learn more."

Amarra stared at her melted footprints behind her. She said, "It's too late."

"No!" Beya leaned forward and reached out, her phantom hand fluttering lightly over Amarra's cheek. "You are untried, child. You need a teacher. I . . . I'm ready, at last, to be your guide."

Amarra was unable to move, unable to respond. She had no more tears, though she could see the pain and fire of the truth on her mother's stricken face. She whispered hoarsely, "We have lost too much. I have to go."

"Why? Why?"

Amarra shook her head. She did not know how to explain. She had no way to show her mother how her heart had been crushed like glass into a fine and cutting powder, in that moment when Beya had wished Death would take her daughter in place of Paudan. That moment had done something to her heart that was so irrevocable it goaded her to flee.

Finally, she said the only good thing she could find in her heart. "You have been my teacher, mother. I have learned. I have learned much."

Beya clenched her hands. For a long time she simply stared at her daughter. A ragged "Yes!" was torn from her before she turned and knelt at the wishing stone. She bowed her head and touched the unpupiled eyes of the owl. Little by little, she lost substance, then disappeared and was gone. In the snow where she had knelt lay two bright silver-mirrored earrings.

Amarra stooped to pick them up. They were cold in her hand and winked like bright eyes in the sunlight. Carefully she put them on and whispered, "I will come home to you, Mother. Someday."

She was alone in the garden of her childhood now. Far off, but clearly, the bells of Trost rang seasonchange, fall to winter. She was not troubled by their tolling. There were no voices in the music to call her name.

"Now," she said aloud. She looked down at the wishing stone and touched the owl's head. The great stone bird woke. Its steady, ancient gaze bore down on her, but this time she did not fear. The owl swiveled its head from side to side, clicked its hollow beak, flapped its powerful wings.

Trembling with the effort, Amarra Snow-Eyes Nie lifted the owl out of the stone, freeing it. The creature stretched its wings full span and danced on her arm in an effort to gain a firm balance. Its talons sliced into her as it shot away from her hand, but the pain did not matter. The owl was no longer a dread creature, but neither was it the childhood companion to whisper secrets to . . . It had become something new to her, just as she was somehow someone new, inside. She watched, panting to keep back a sob, as the owl glided silent above her head and then rose up over the rooftop, flying off toward the sea.

Notes

This is a phonetical rendering of the alphabet of the first language of Gueame. It is no longer spoken in the southern Kieldings. In the eastern Kieldings, it is still spoken by the Ebsters, a group of religious who live in Mossdon Kield.

Phonetic renderings of the inscription in the alcoves of Trost's villa:

à	(	l	(
ě	⌐	m	(
î	~	n	(
ō	⌐	p	··
û	∂	r	ⱳ
y	ⱱ	s	?
		t	∫
b	c	v	·
c	∫	w	ⱺ
d	()		
f	L	x	ⱶ
g	?	z	⌐
h	?		
j	ⱴ	ch	ⱳⱳ
k	ⱶ	sc	ⱱ
		gh	Ɒ

Gwaněs wōěs sěf

?⌐(ⱱ-?⌐ⱳ-??-ⱶ

223